RICHARD VAN CAMP   SCOTT B. HENDERSON   DONOVAN YACIUK

The SPIRIT of DENENDEH

VOLUME 1

A BLANKET OF BUTTERFLIES

HIGHWATER PRESS

The most powerful words in any writer's tool kit are: "What if?"

A Blanket of Butterflies has a simple origin: my buddy, James Croizier—a security guard at the Northern Lights Museum in my hometown of Fort Smith, NWT—kept telling me about a suit of samurai armour at the museum. Knowing that I was fascinated with ninjas and samurai culture, he encouraged me to visit the museum and see the armour for myself. I didn't believe him until one day, Mr. Currie—a curator at the museum—said it was true and that he'd be happy to open the boxes housing the armour for me. I still didn't believe it until the next day when I saw the armour for myself. Then I thought, *what if?*

What if a man from Japan (Shinobu) came to retrieve this armour to redeem himself and his family's honour? *What if* the dangerous men I write about in my short stories (Torchy, Sfen, Flinch, Benny the Bank) tried to stop him?

What if a young man (Sonny) wanted to help Shinobu, and that young man was raised by his grandmother (Ehtsi)? *What if* she knew the words of a sacred story that could stop the escalating violence?

What if I used this story to honour Ayah, the prophet of Deline? *What if* I passed along the story that Sahtu Dene author and storyteller George Blondin shared with my class when I was studying at Arctic College in Yellowknife about how Ayah foresaw the bombs that would drop over Hiroshima and Nagasaki? *What if* I honoured Ayah and Mr. Blondin through this story while creating space for youth and the world to read our Dene Laws?

That's how the story came together—through a powerful series of *what-ifs.*

After writing the story, I had the joy of working with artist Scott Henderson. Scott took the story to a whole new level. Check out that splash page of the fight between Torchy, Sfen, and Shinobu. Check out the dirty boxing and the martial arts the brothers were trained in called "The Dance of Pain." Only Scott could turn six pages of writing into a two-page spread showcasing all of this.

Suddenly, this story of *what-ifs* became a shortlisted, Eisner Award–nominated reality. As a comics collector of over 40 years, this is one of the highest honours I've received in my writing career.

I'd like to dedicate this comic to Mr. James Crozier, my adopted brother and lifelong friend. Thank you, James, for telling me about the armour. I'd also like to honour Scott Henderson for his work here. It's some of his finest, and I am a huge fan of his. I'd also like to thank Donovan Yaciuk, whose magnificent colouration brought a new spirit and energy to this story. Thank you also to Nickolej Villiger, who did an outstanding job bringing the soundscape of the story to life through his lettering.

I'm excited for you to see what's coming up next in The Spirit of Denendeh series. We have even more magic planned with Benny, Crow, Torchy, Sfen, Flinch, and a few new characters we hope you will love and root for. And the best part for me? It's set in my hometown of Fort Smith, NWT: my heartland. Mahsi cho, HighWater Press, for giving me, my friends, and my heroes a platform to create the graphic novels of our dreams. I want to thank my editor, Irene Velentzas, for helping me take this story to where it has always wanted to be. Mahsi cho!

To learn more about the mysterious armour that inspired this story, visit CBC.ca and search for Jacob Barker's article, "Suit of armour remains a mystery for Fort Smith, N.W.T., museum," posted on December 30, 2014.

What you are holding now is my imagined version of how this mysterious suit of samurai armour found its way to my hometown and how it returned to its rightful home through the power and grace of a Dene matriarch.

Mahsi cho, everyone. I am grateful. I am inspired.

Mahsi cho.

Richard Van Camp
Under the full moon of October 2021

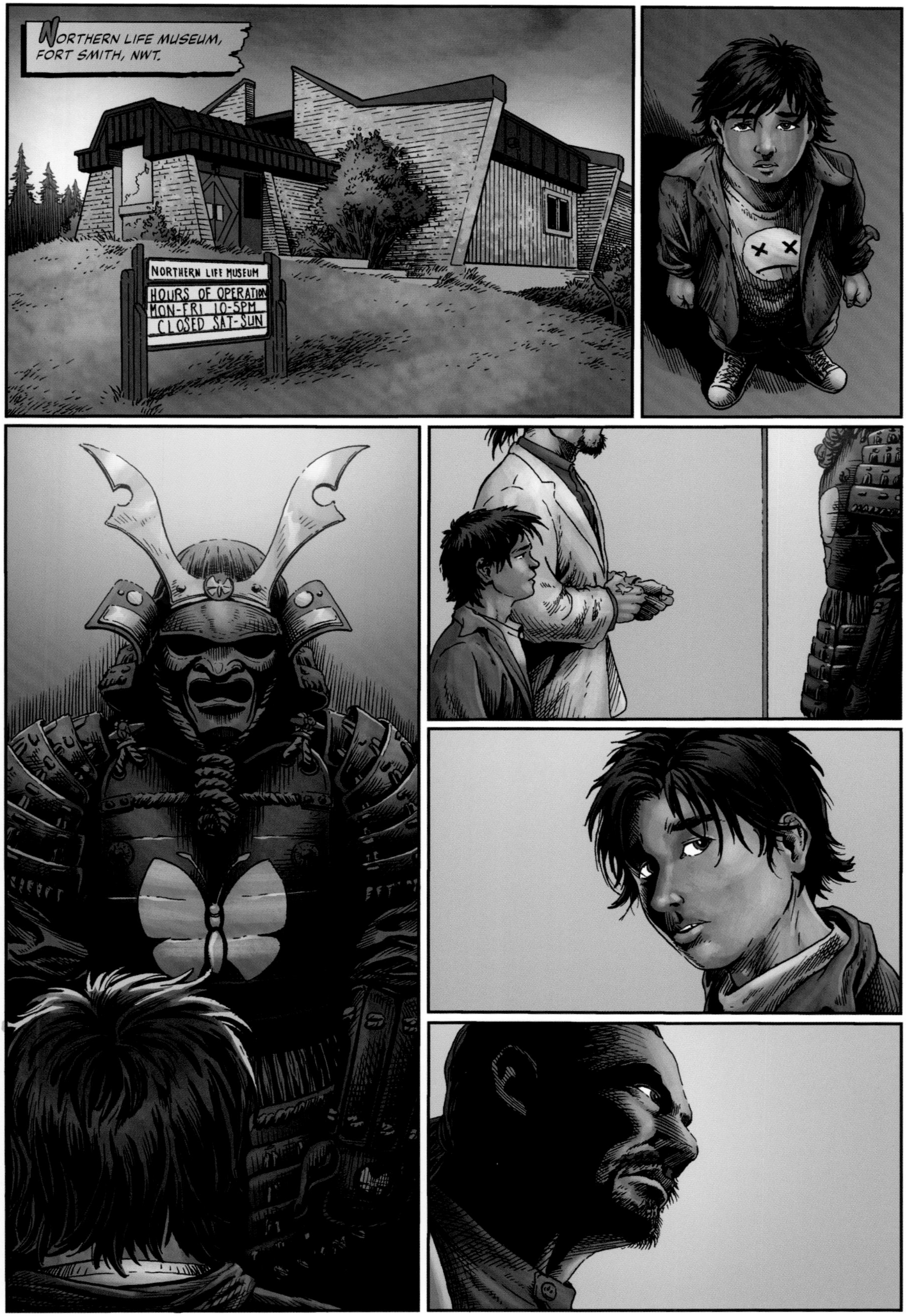
Northern life museum,
fort smith, NWT.
NORTHERN LIFE MUSEUM
HOURS OF OPERATION
MON-FRI 10-5PM
CLOSED SAT-SUN

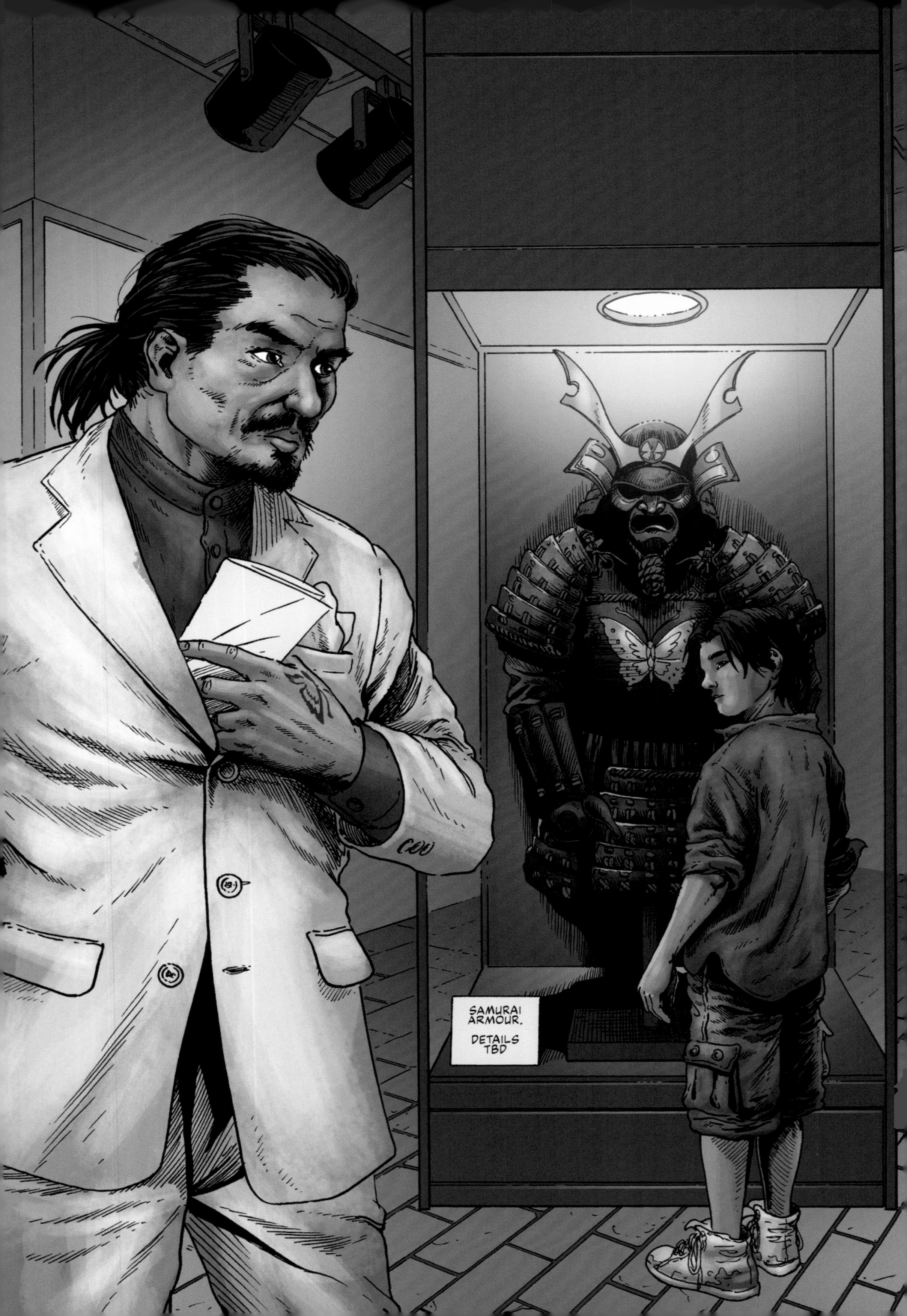
SAMURAI ARMOUR.
DETAILS TBD

GOOD DAY TO YOU, SIR.

I AM SHINOBU. WE SPOKE ON THE PHONE?

HELLO, MR. SHINOBU.

THANK YOU FOR COMING ALL THIS WAY. WE ARE HONOURED THAT THIS SUIT IS RETURNING TO YOUR FAMILY.

YES, WE THINK THE SUIT WAS MEANT FOR THE MUSEUM IN FORT SMITH, ARKANSAS. NOT FORT SMITH, NWT.

WHERE IS THE SWORD?

...

WELL, NOW, HERE'S THE PROBLEM...

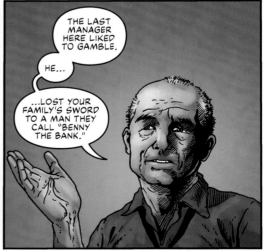

THE LAST MANAGER HERE LIKED TO GAMBLE.

HE...

...LOST YOUR FAMILY'S SWORD TO A MAN THEY CALL "BENNY THE BANK."

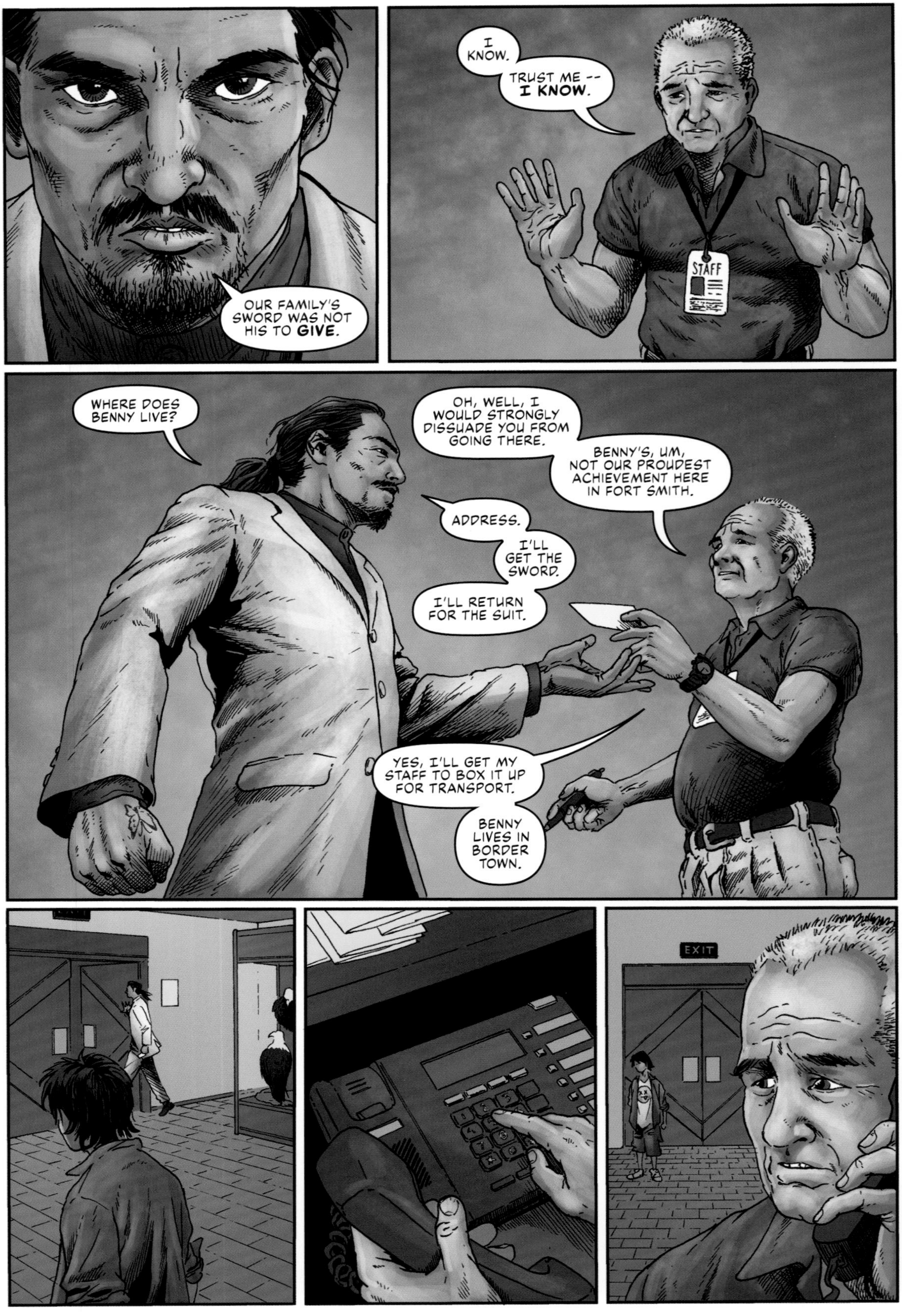
OUR FAMILY'S SWORD WAS NOT HIS TO GIVE.
I KNOW.
TRUST ME -- I KNOW.
WHERE DOES BENNY LIVE?
OH, WELL, I WOULD STRONGLY DISSUADE YOU FROM GOING THERE.
BENNY'S, UM, NOT OUR PROUDEST ACHIEVEMENT HERE IN FORT SMITH.
ADDRESS.
I'LL GET THE SWORD.
I'LL RETURN FOR THE SUIT.
YES, I'LL GET MY STAFF TO BOX IT UP FOR TRANSPORT.
BENNY LIVES IN BORDER TOWN.
STAFF
EXIT

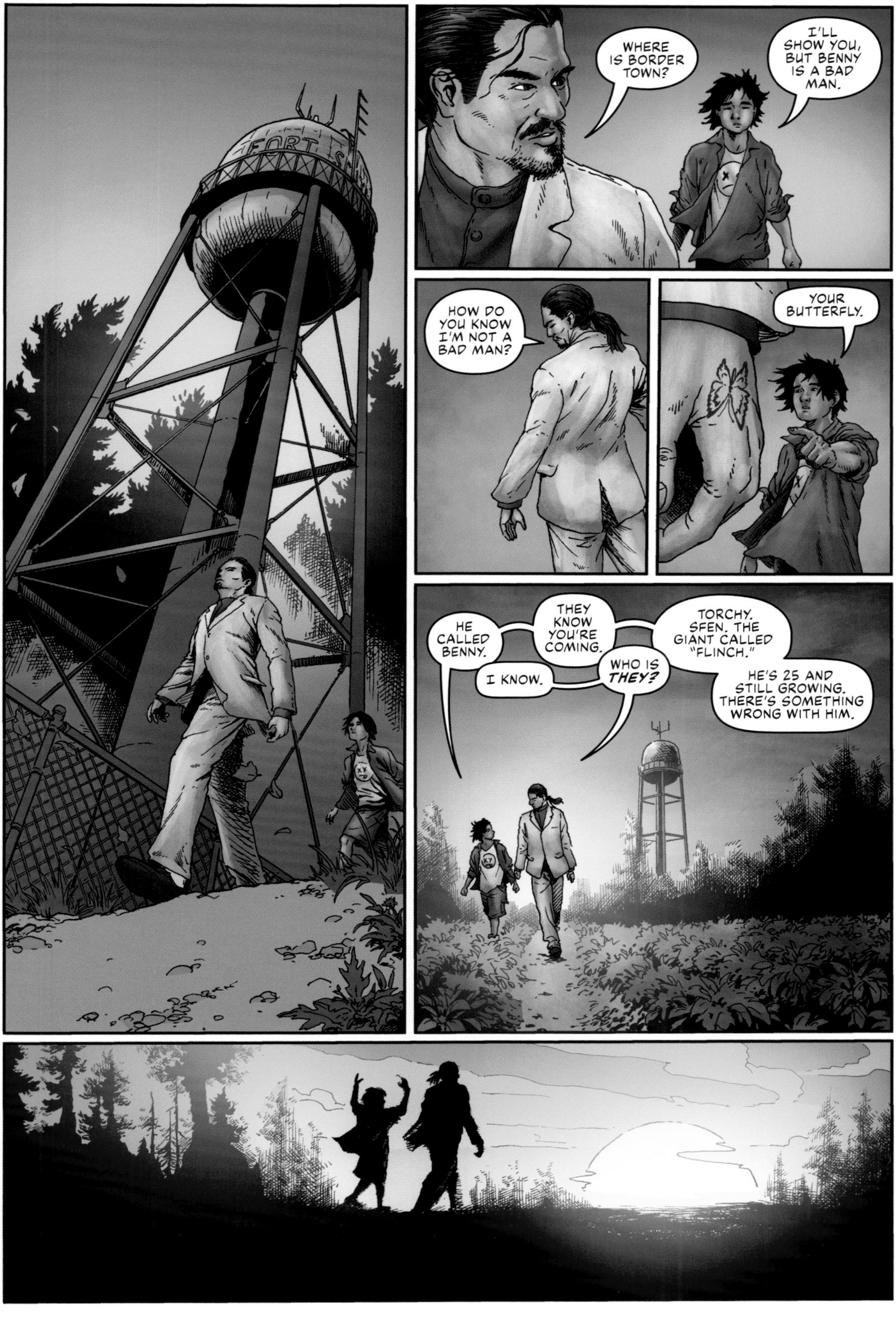
FORT S
WHERE IS BORDER TOWN?
I'LL SHOW YOU, BUT BENNY IS A BAD MAN.
HOW DO YOU KNOW I'M NOT A BAD MAN?
YOUR BUTTERFLY.
HE CALLED BENNY.
THEY KNOW YOU'RE COMING.
I KNOW.
WHO IS *THEY?*
TORCHY. SFEN. THE GIANT CALLED "FLINCH."
HE'S 25 AND STILL GROWING. THERE'S SOMETHING WRONG WITH HIM.

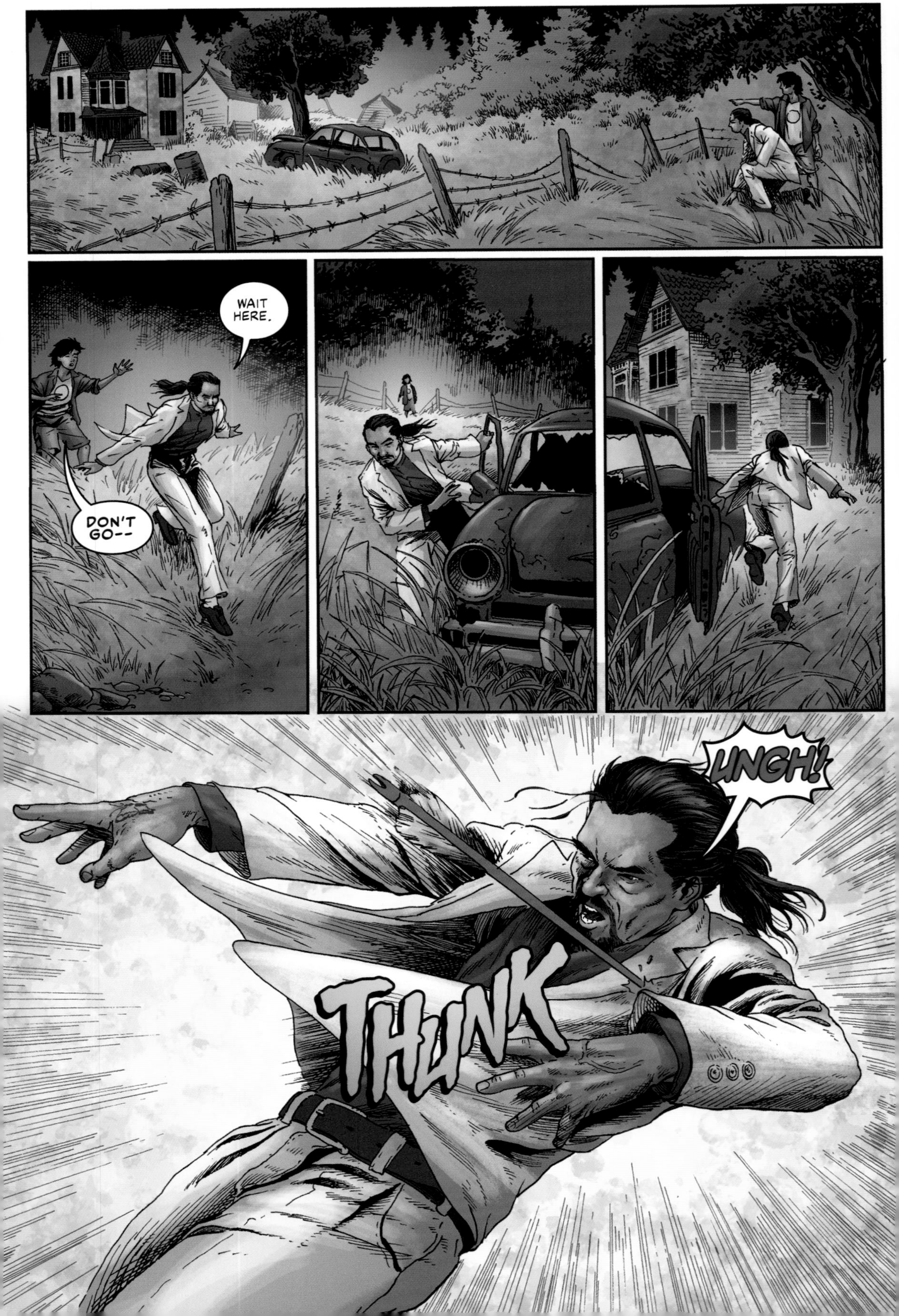
WAIT HERE.
DON'T GO--
UNGH!
THUNK

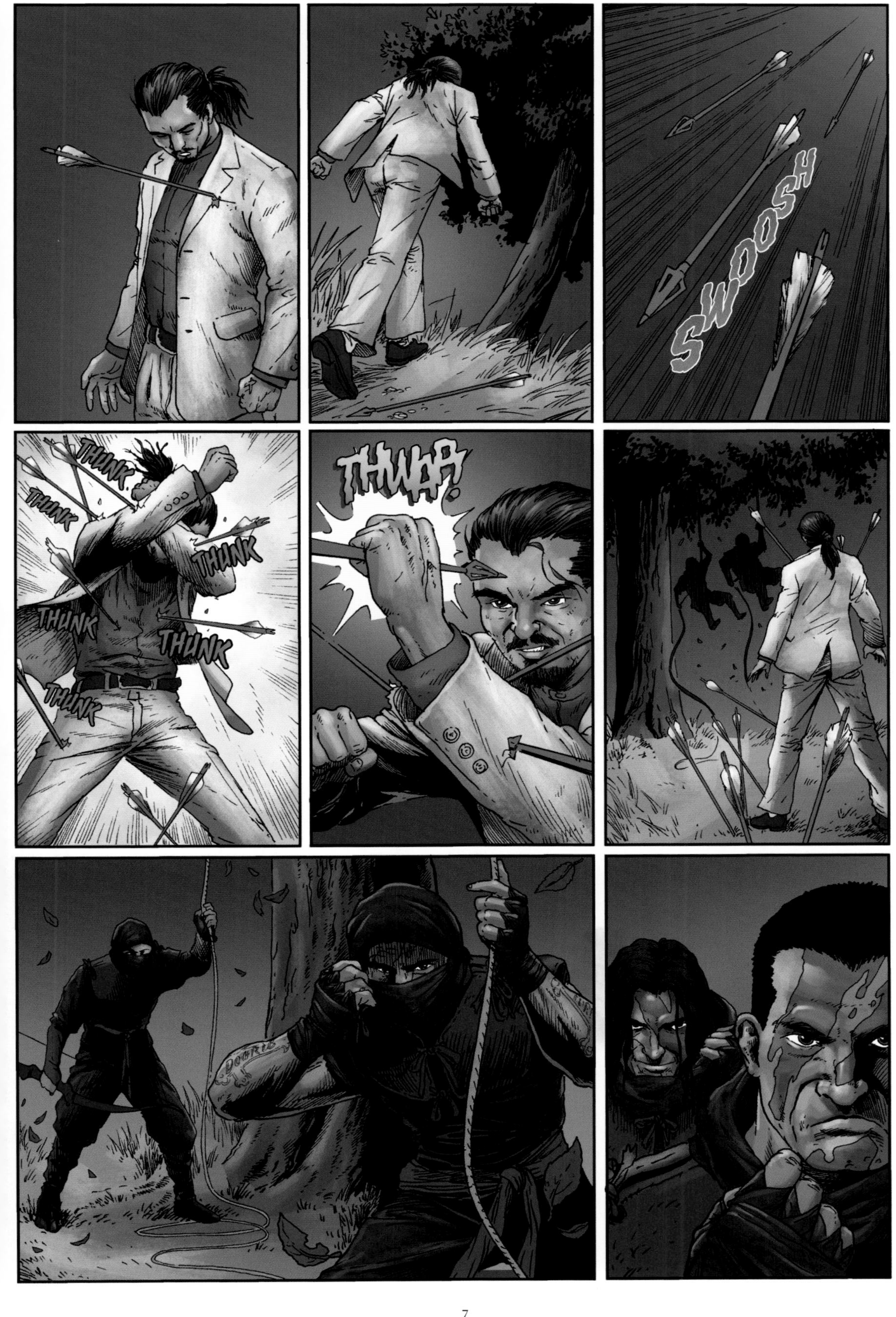
SWOOSH
THUNK
THUNK
THUNK
THUNK
THUNK
THUNK
THWAP!

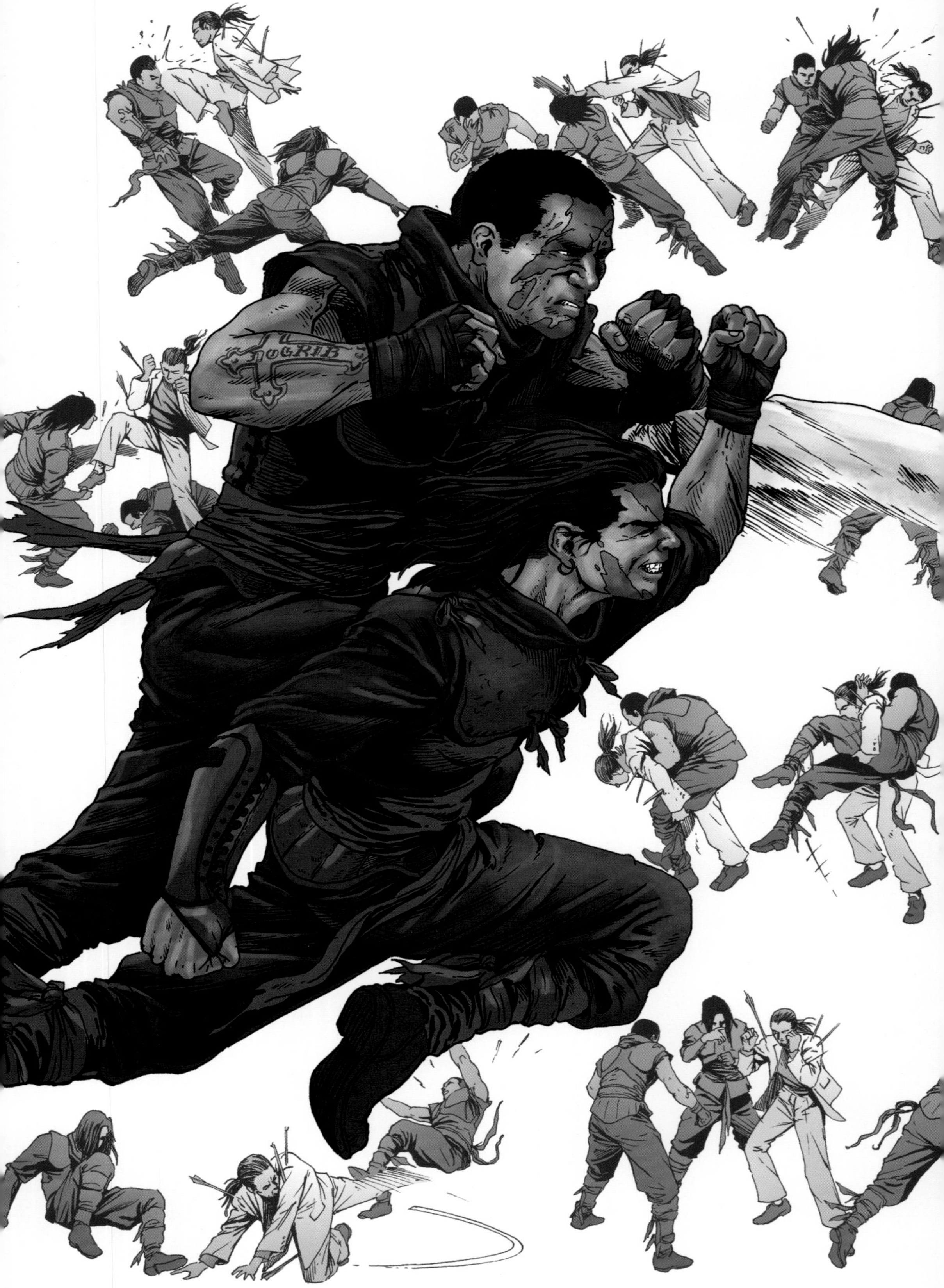

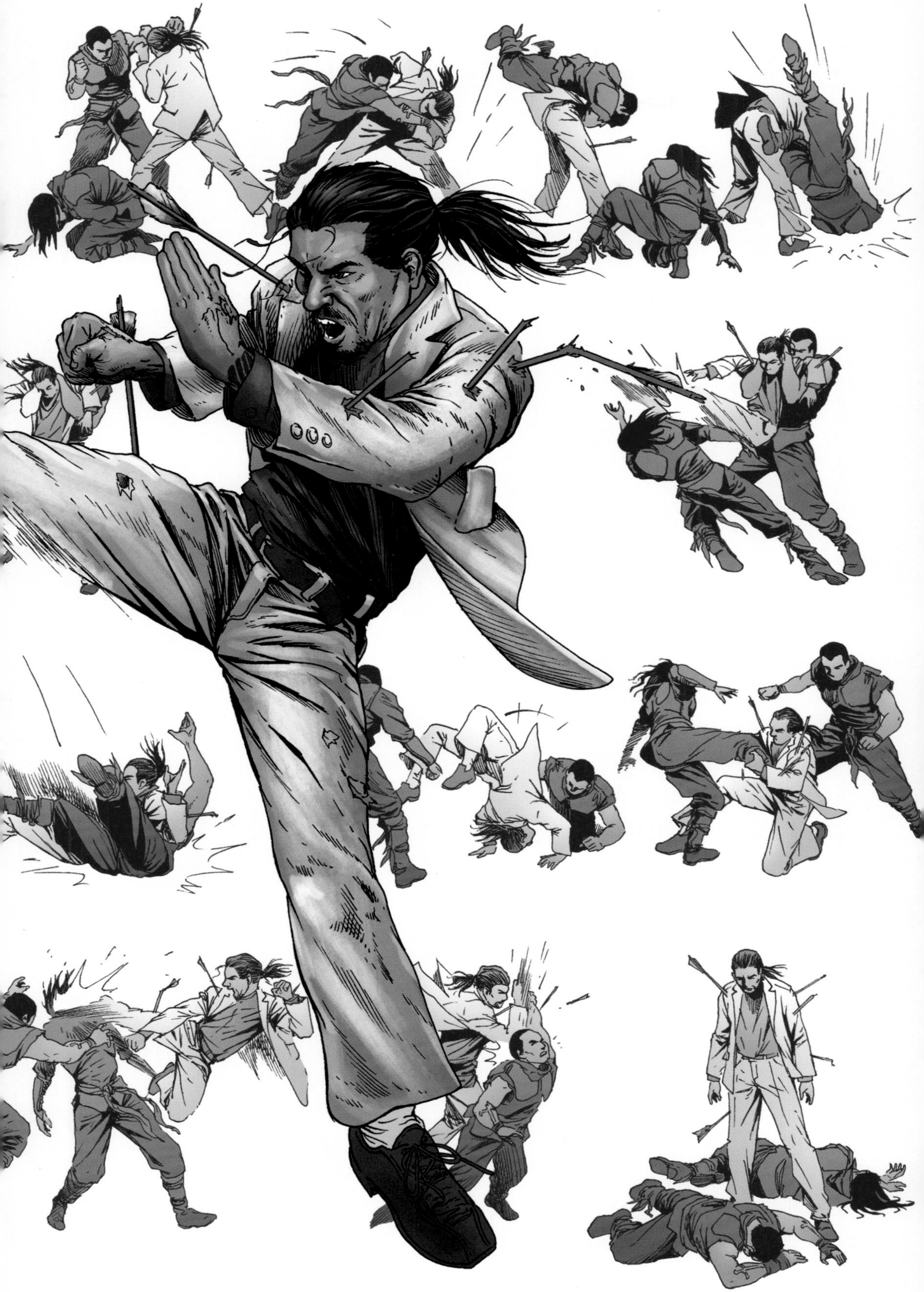

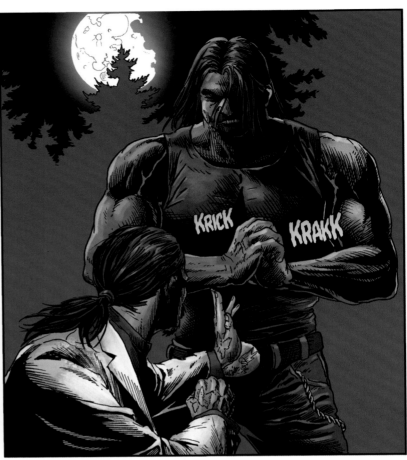

KRICK

KRAKK

THUNK

THWAK

CRACK

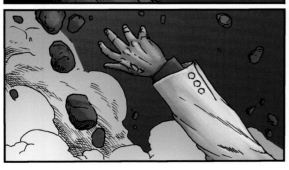

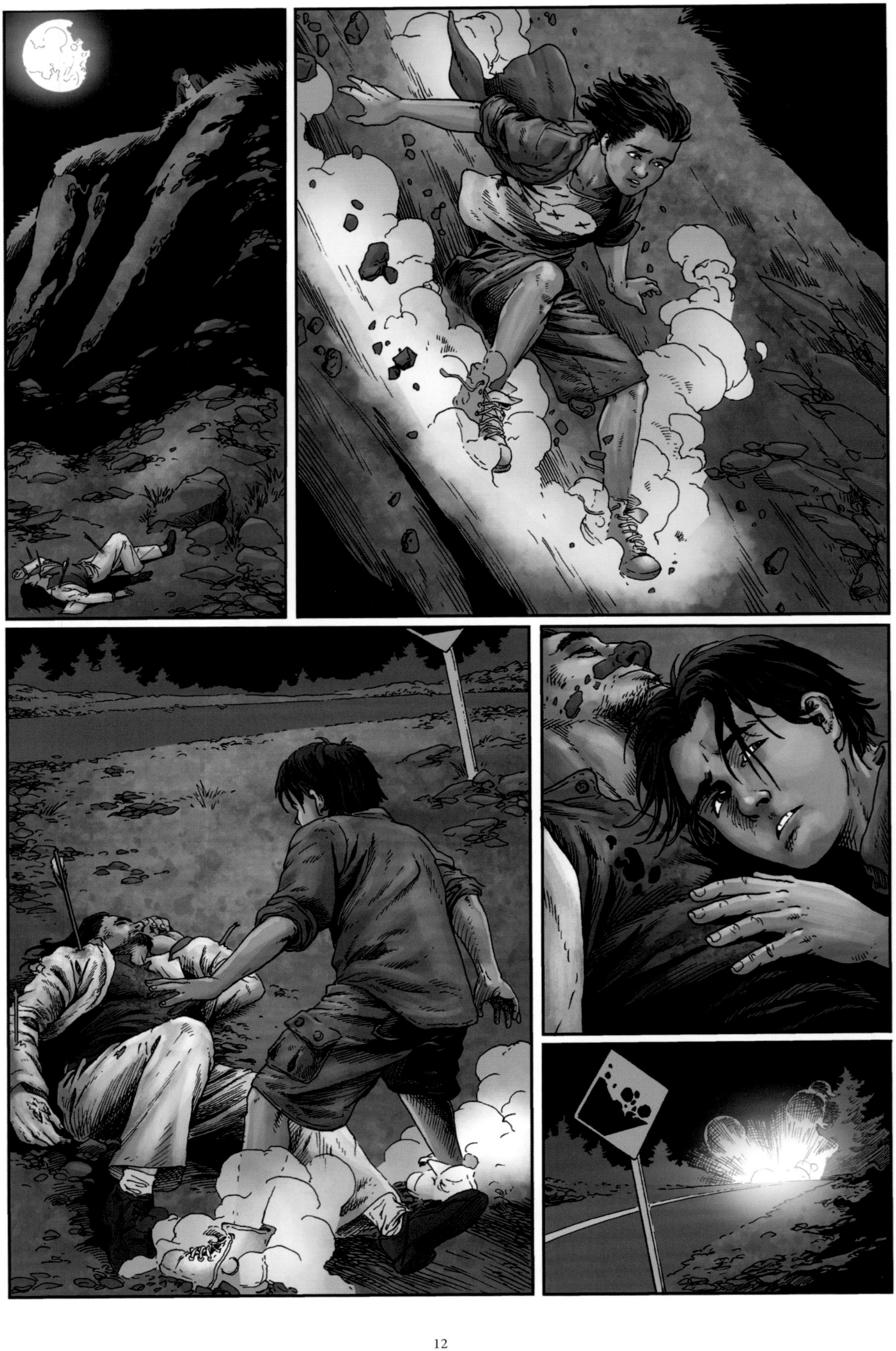

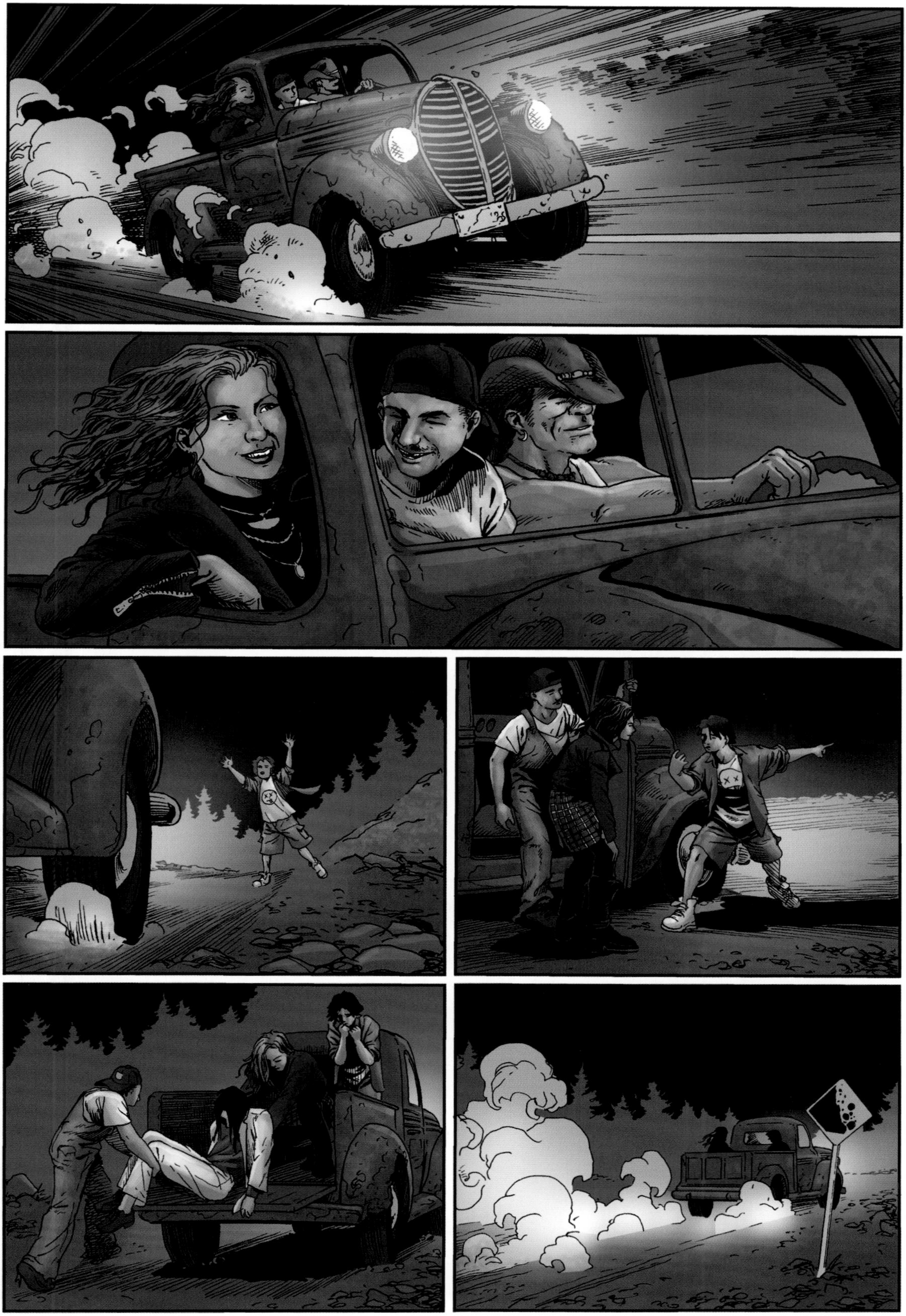

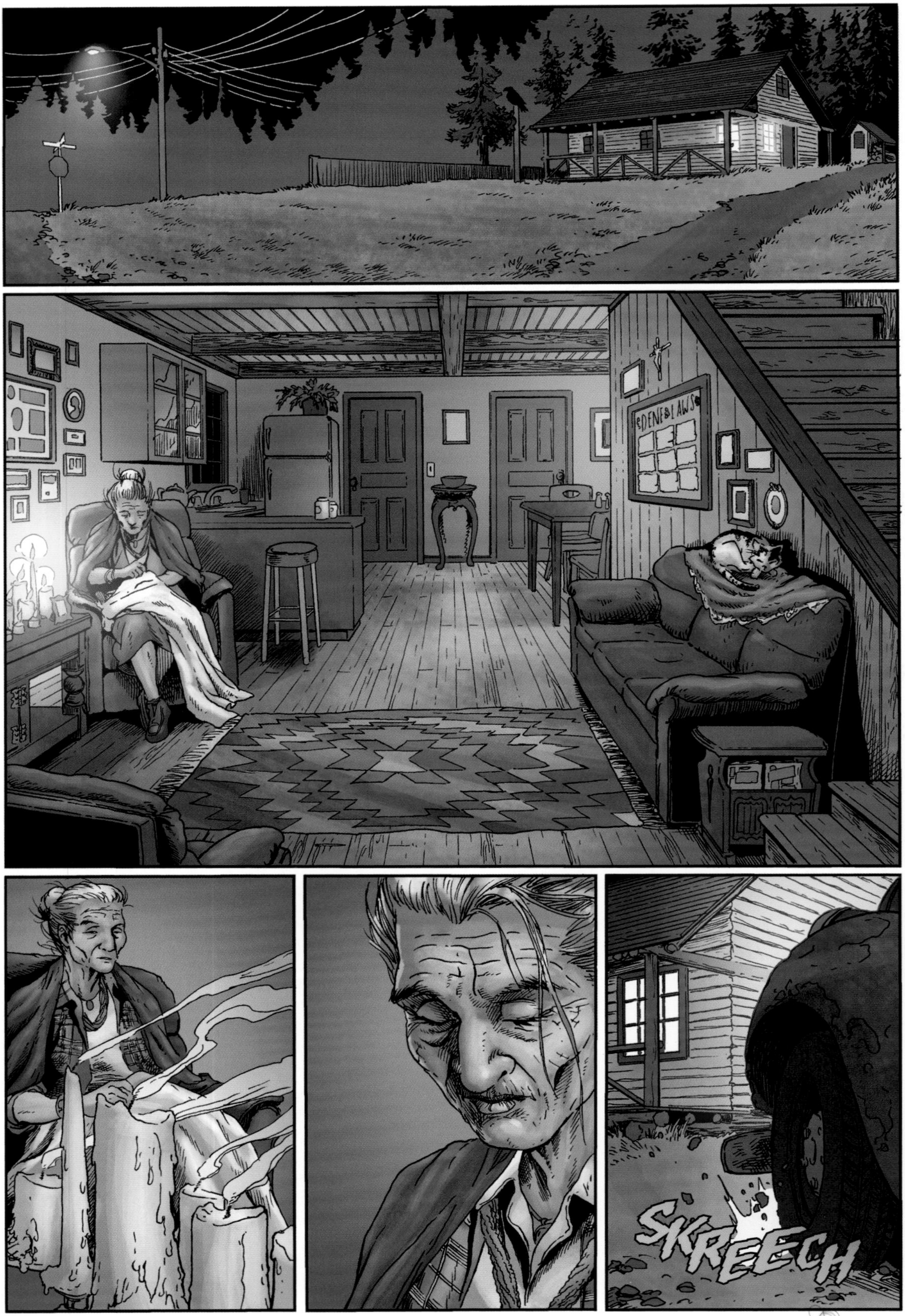
DENE LAWS
SKREECH

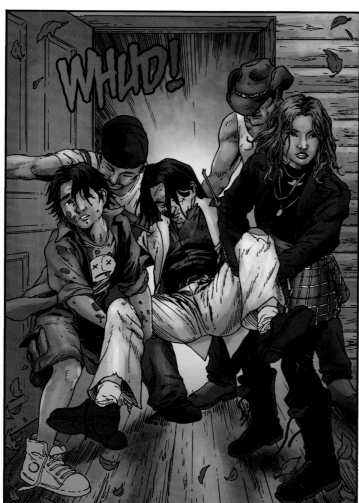

WHUD!

PUT HIM HERE.

SONNY, WHAT HAPPENED? AH MI NAY?*

*WHO IS THIS? TRANSLATED FROM TŁĮCHǪ.

HELP HIM. **PLEASE**, EHTSI.*

*GRANDMOTHER.

GO. KEEP THIS A SECRET.

OKAY, AUNTY. LOVE YOU.

LOVE YOU, TOO, MY GIRL.

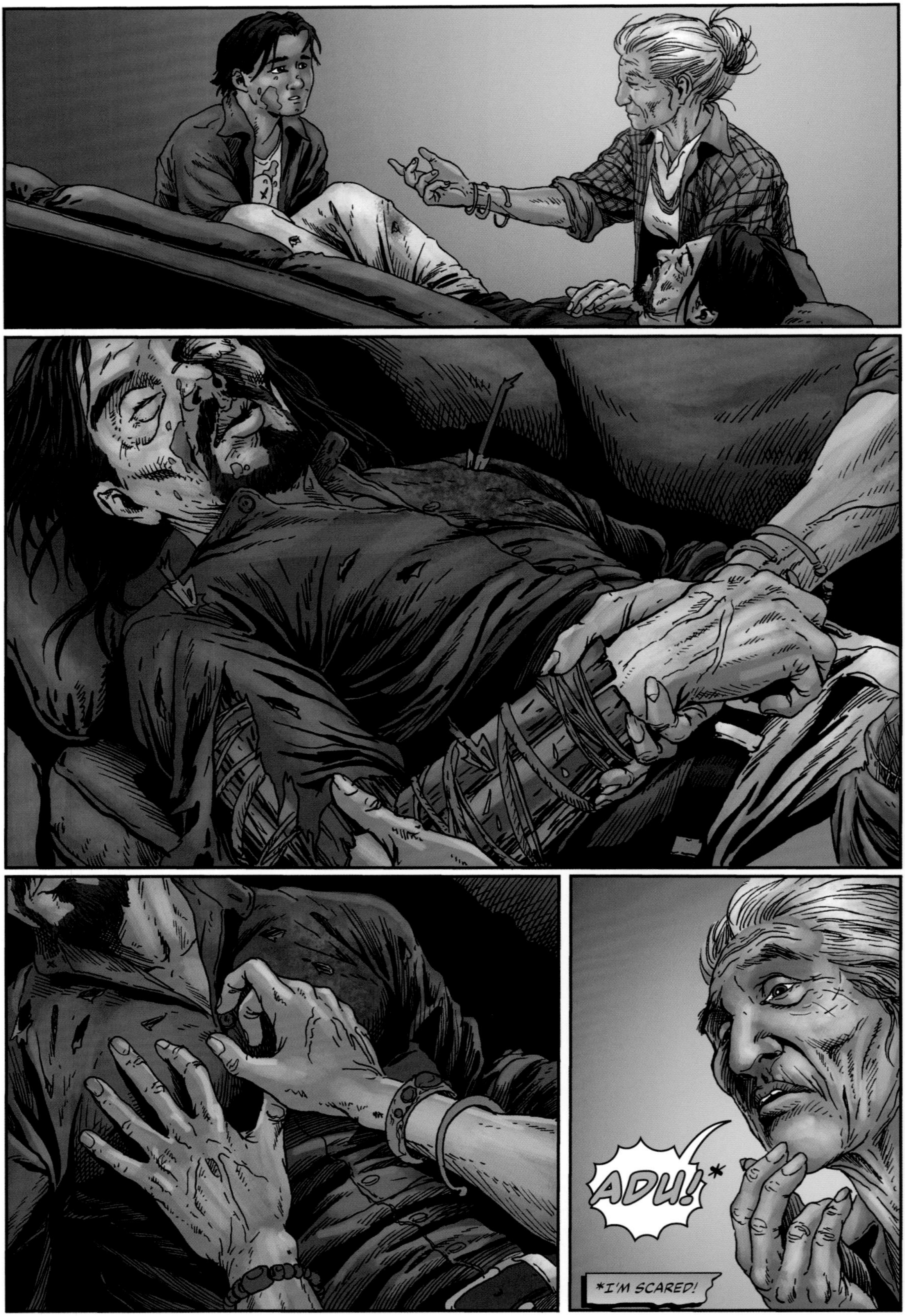
ADU!*
*I'M SCARED!

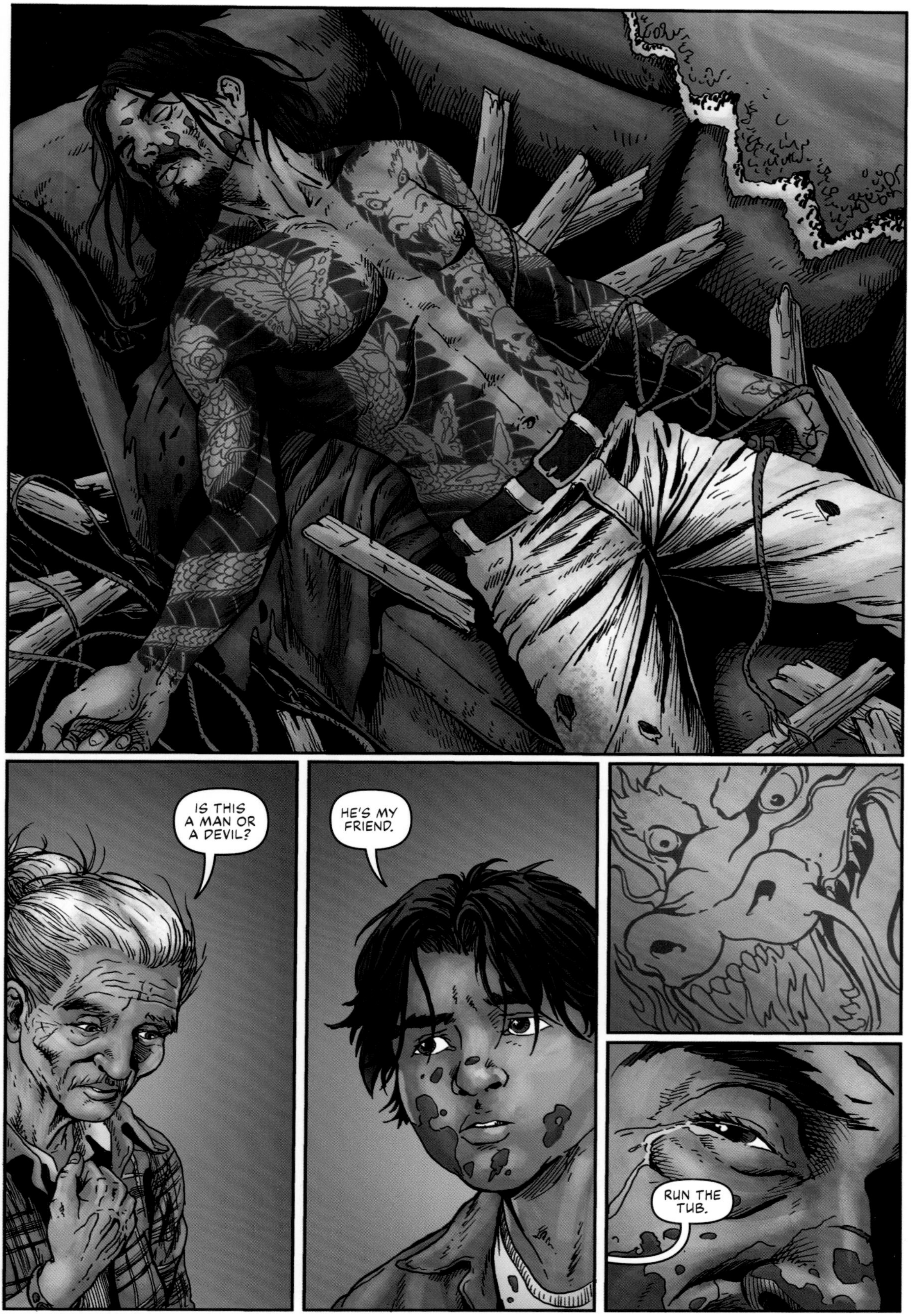
IS THIS A MAN OR A DEVIL?
HE'S MY FRIEND.
RUN THE TUB.

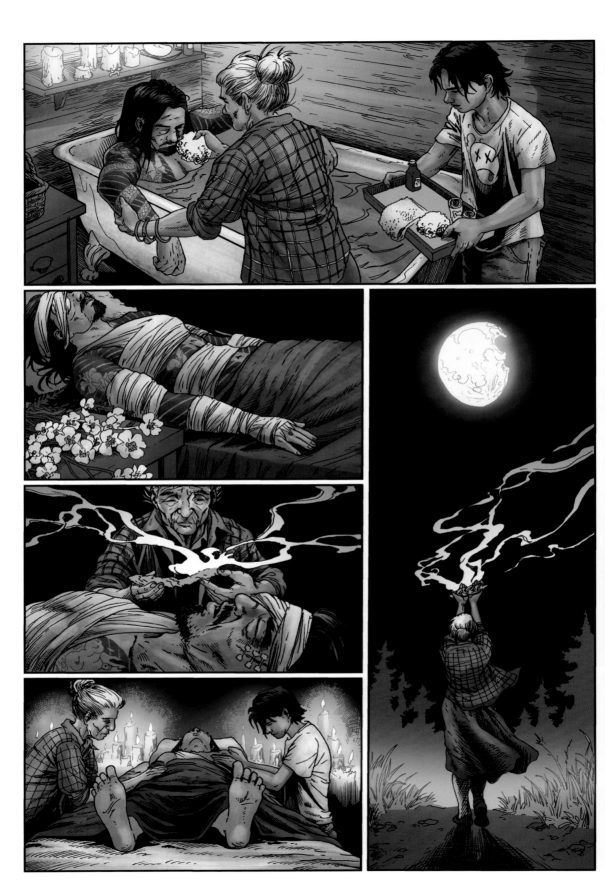

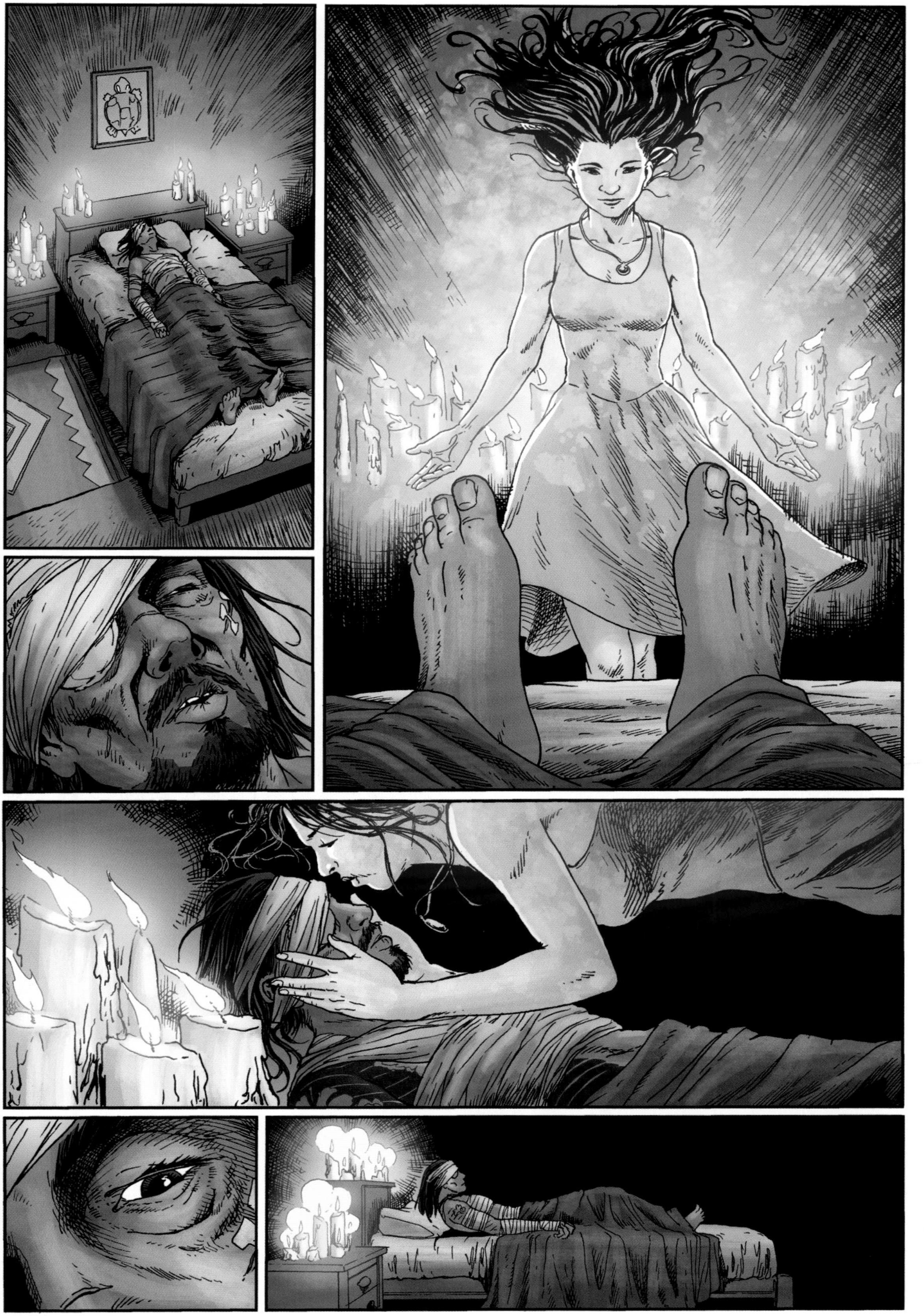

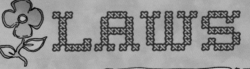

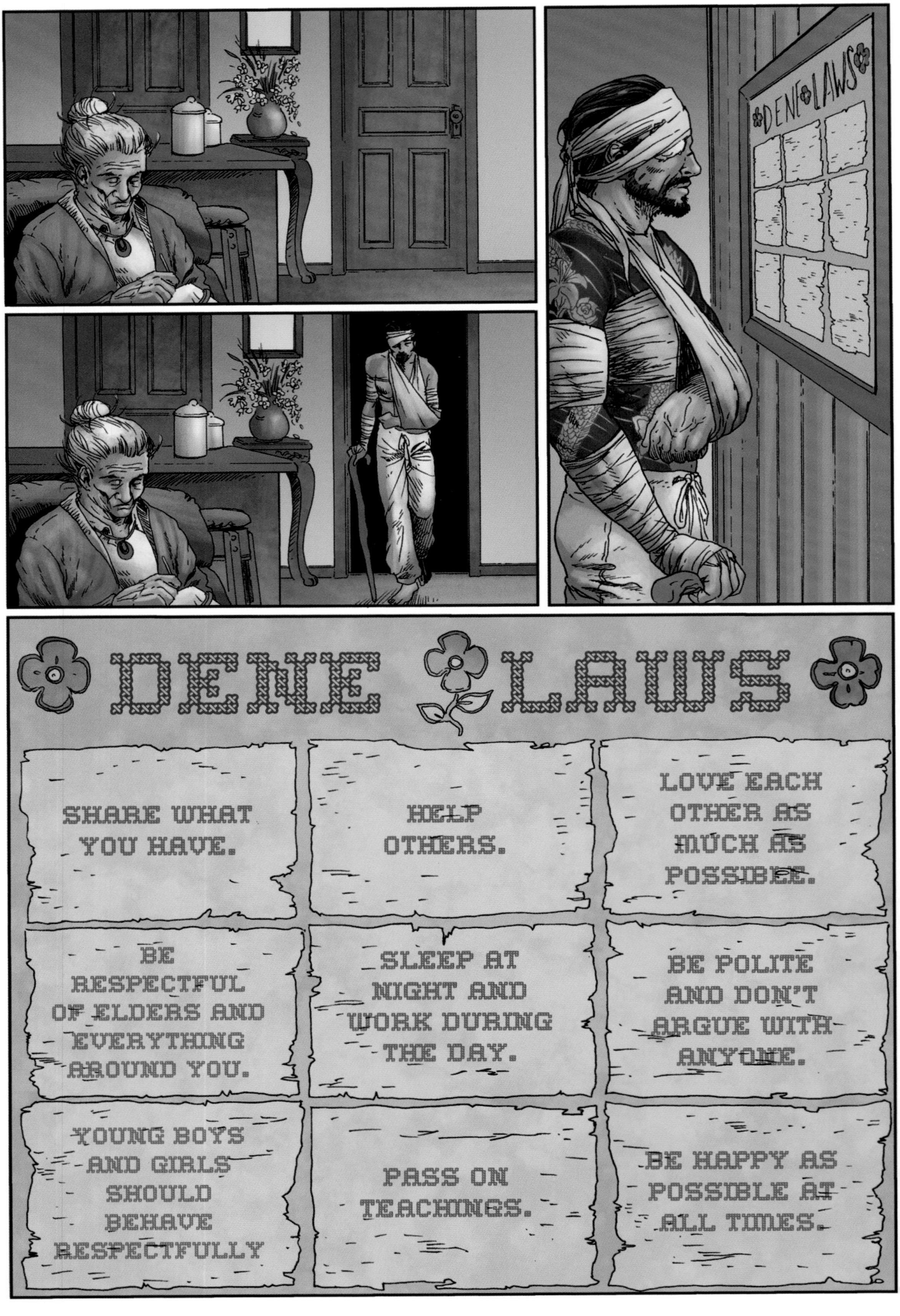

DENE ☙ LAWS

SHARE WHAT YOU HAVE.	HELP OTHERS.	LOVE EACH OTHER AS MUCH AS POSSIBLE.
BE RESPECTFUL OF ELDERS AND EVERYTHING AROUND YOU.	SLEEP AT NIGHT AND WORK DURING THE DAY.	BE POLITE AND DON'T ARGUE WITH ANYONE.
YOUNG BOYS AND GIRLS SHOULD BEHAVE RESPECTFULLY	PASS ON TEACHINGS.	BE HAPPY AS POSSIBLE AT ALL TIMES.

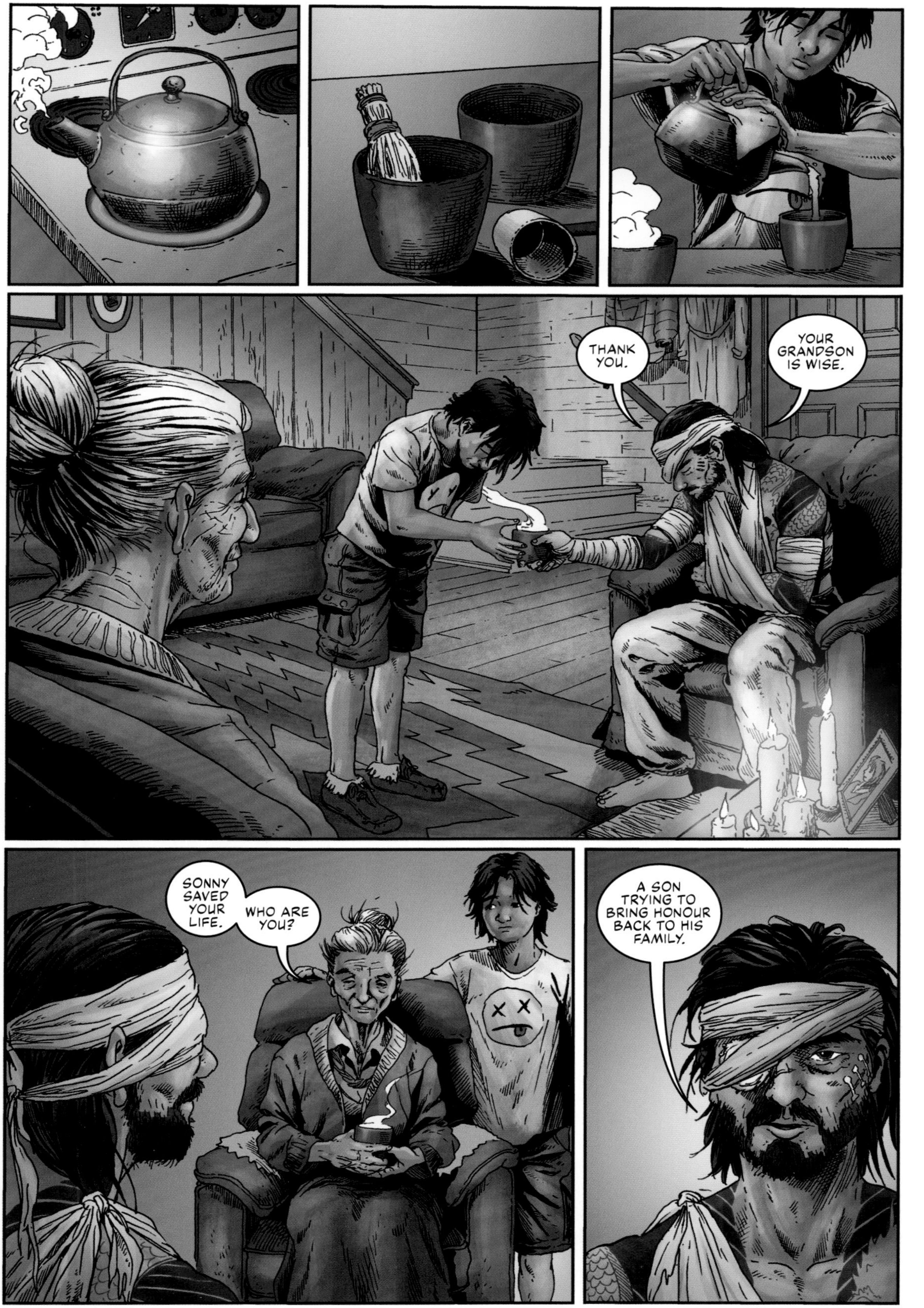
THANK YOU.
YOUR GRANDSON IS WISE.
SONNY SAVED YOUR LIFE.
WHO ARE YOU?
A SON TRYING TO BRING HONOUR BACK TO HIS FAMILY.

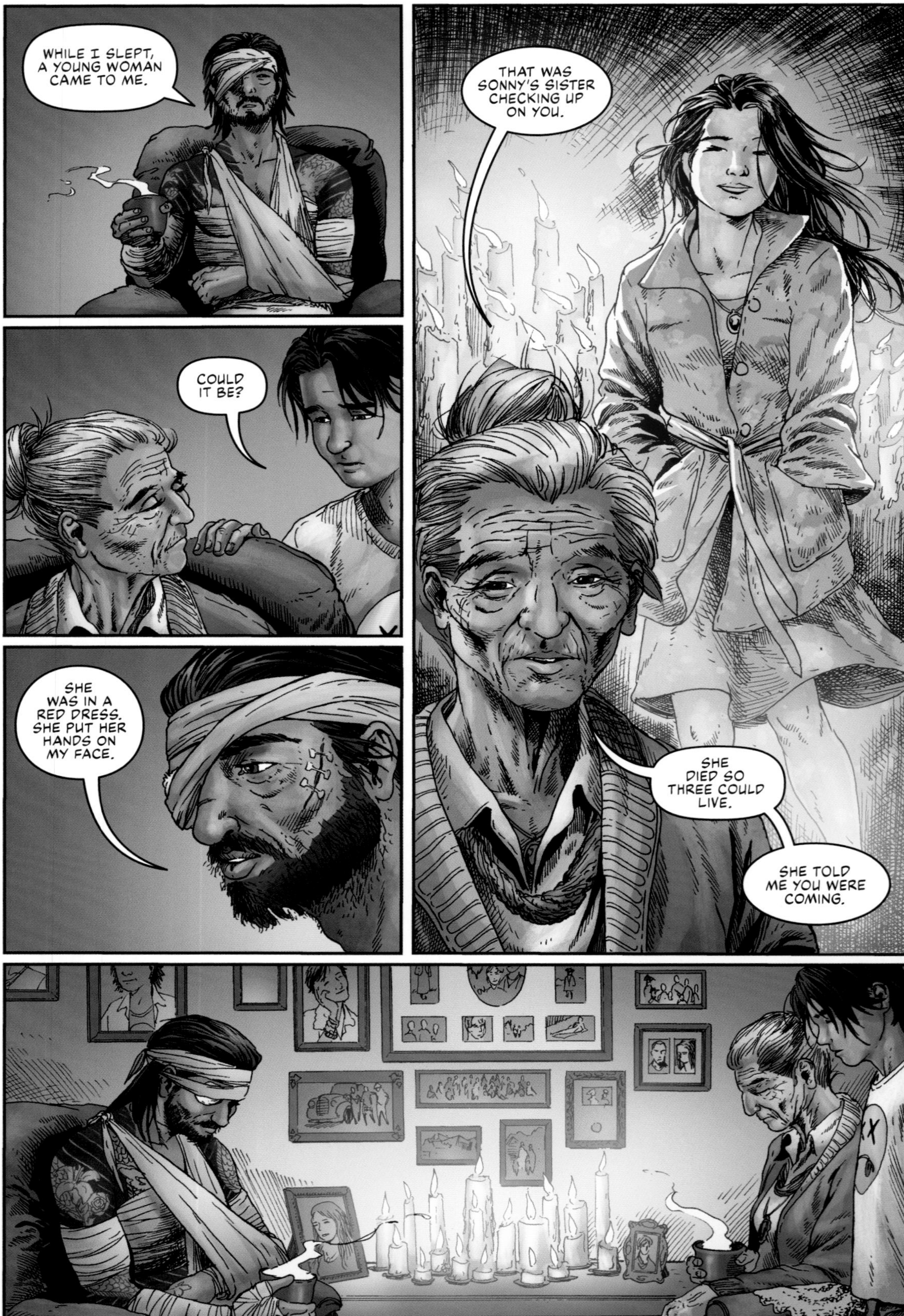
WHILE I SLEPT, A YOUNG WOMAN CAME TO ME.
COULD IT BE?
SHE WAS IN A RED DRESS. SHE PUT HER HANDS ON MY FACE.
THAT WAS SONNY'S SISTER CHECKING UP ON YOU.
SHE DIED SO THREE COULD LIVE.
SHE TOLD ME YOU WERE COMING.

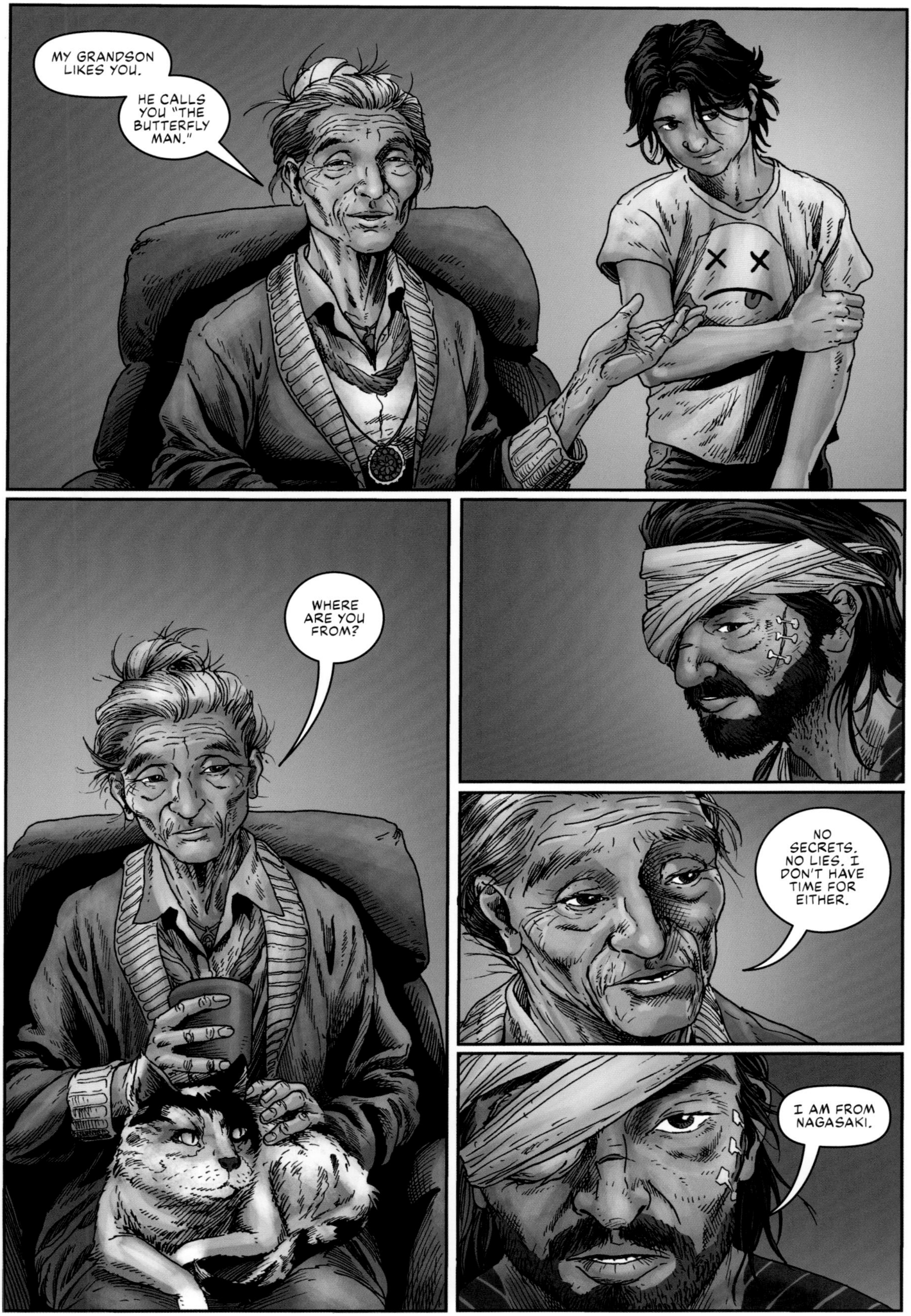
MY GRANDSON LIKES YOU.
HE CALLS YOU "THE BUTTERFLY MAN."
WHERE ARE YOU FROM?
NO SECRETS. NO LIES. I DON'T HAVE TIME FOR EITHER.
I AM FROM NAGASAKI.

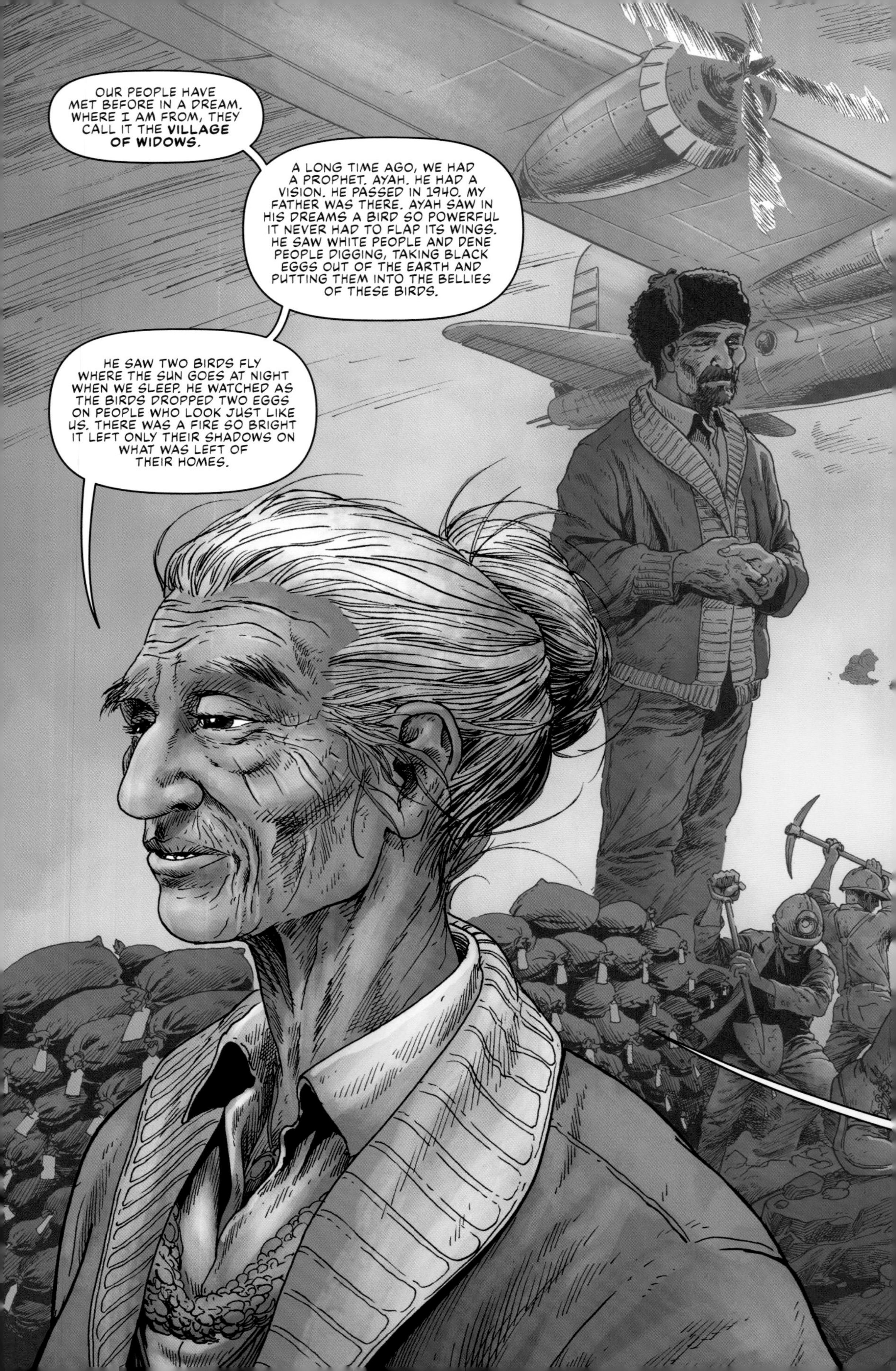
OUR PEOPLE HAVE MET BEFORE IN A DREAM. WHERE I AM FROM, THEY CALL IT THE **VILLAGE OF WIDOWS.**
A LONG TIME AGO, WE HAD A PROPHET. AYAH. HE HAD A VISION. HE PASSED IN 1940. MY FATHER WAS THERE. AYAH SAW IN HIS DREAMS A BIRD SO POWERFUL IT NEVER HAD TO FLAP ITS WINGS. HE SAW WHITE PEOPLE AND DENE PEOPLE DIGGING, TAKING BLACK EGGS OUT OF THE EARTH AND PUTTING THEM INTO THE BELLIES OF THESE BIRDS.
HE SAW TWO BIRDS FLY WHERE THE SUN GOES AT NIGHT WHEN WE SLEEP. HE WATCHED AS THE BIRDS DROPPED TWO EGGS ON PEOPLE WHO LOOK JUST LIKE US. THERE WAS A FIRE SO BRIGHT IT LEFT ONLY THEIR SHADOWS ON WHAT WAS LEFT OF THEIR HOMES.

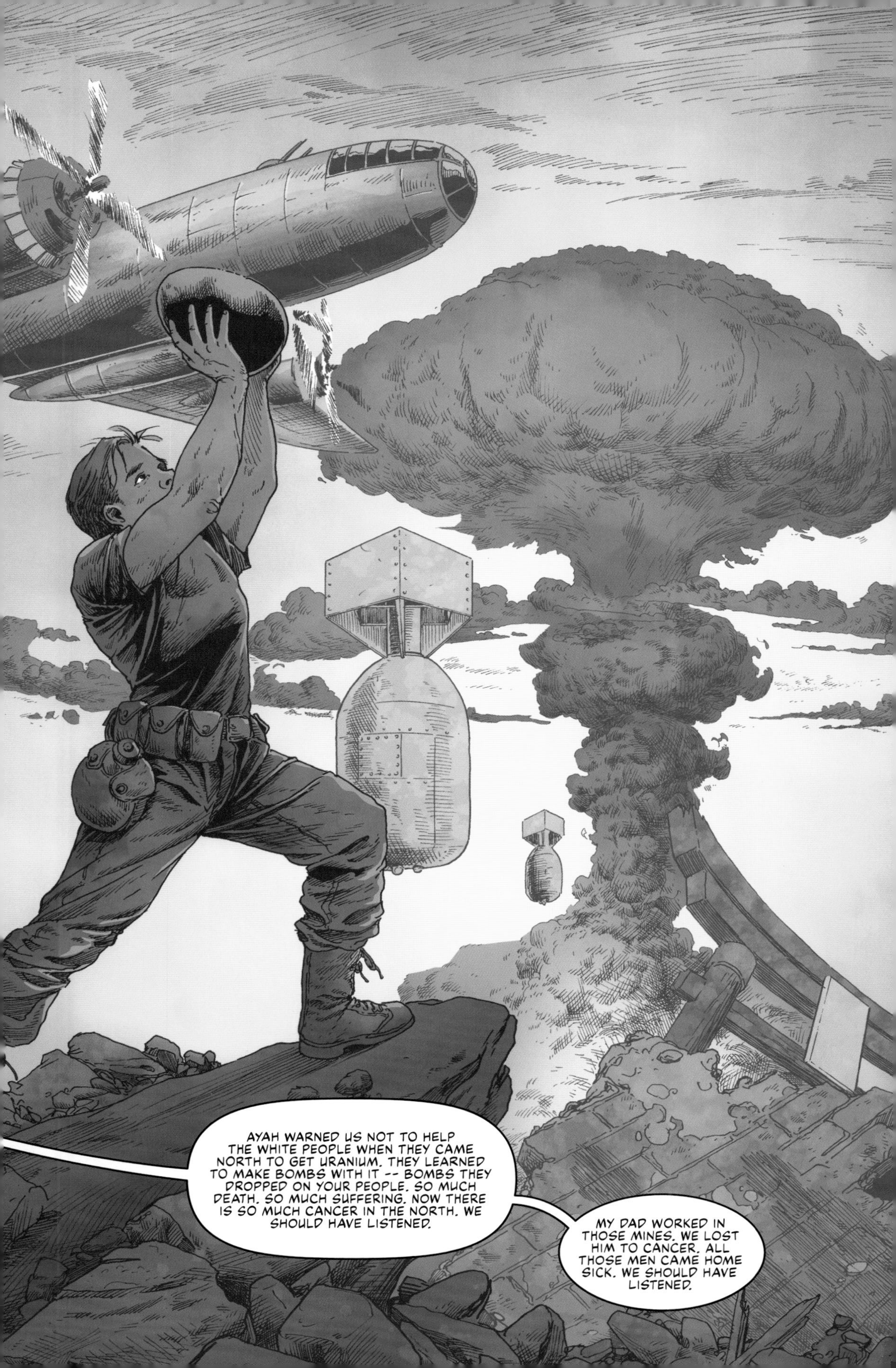
AYAH WARNED US NOT TO HELP THE WHITE PEOPLE WHEN THEY CAME NORTH TO GET URANIUM. THEY LEARNED TO MAKE BOMBS WITH IT -- BOMBS THEY DROPPED ON YOUR PEOPLE. SO MUCH DEATH. SO MUCH SUFFERING. NOW THERE IS SO MUCH CANCER IN THE NORTH. WE SHOULD HAVE LISTENED.
MY DAD WORKED IN THOSE MINES. WE LOST HIM TO CANCER. ALL THOSE MEN CAME HOME SICK. WE SHOULD HAVE LISTENED.

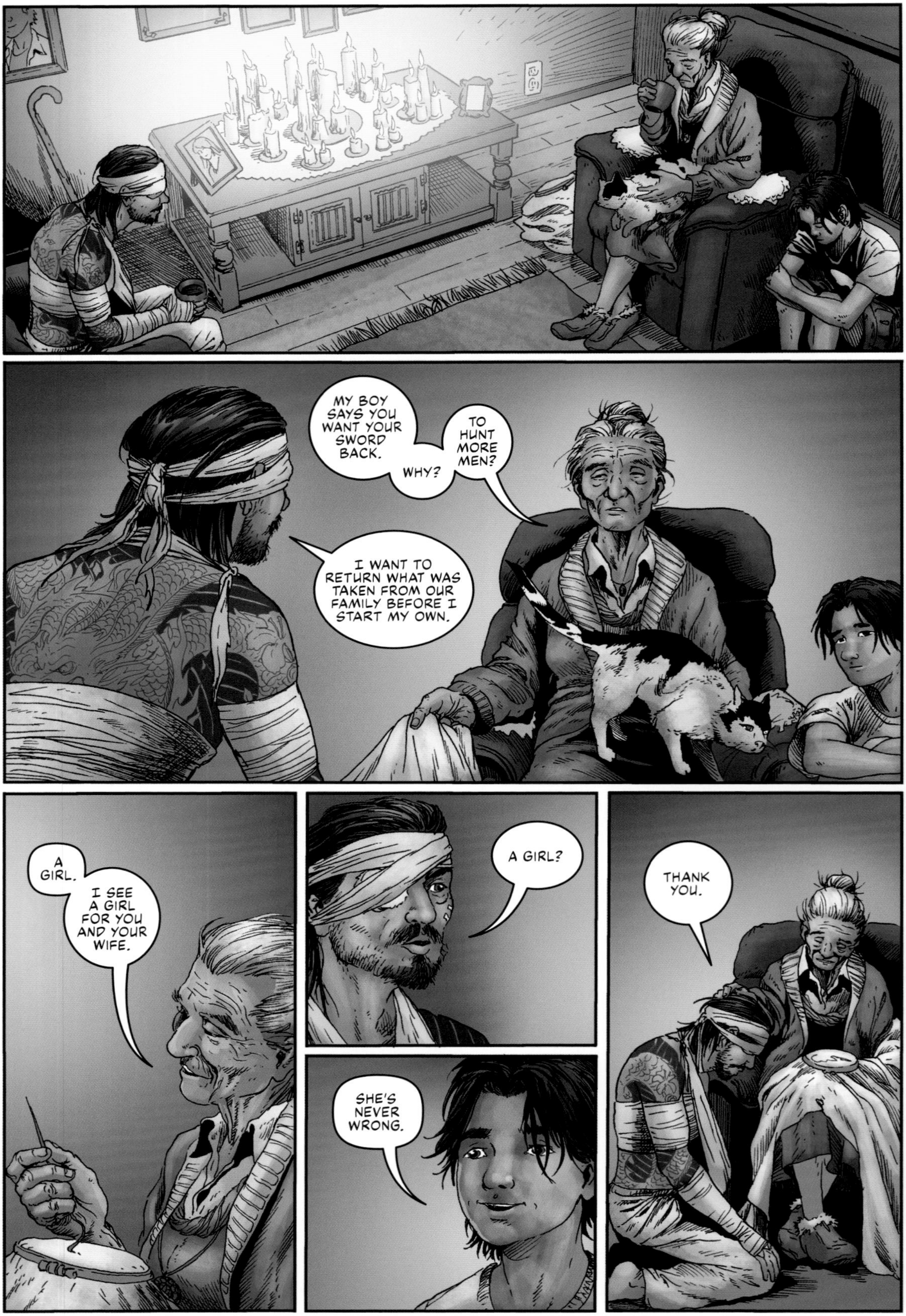
MY BOY SAYS YOU WANT YOUR SWORD BACK.
WHY?
TO HUNT MORE MEN?
I WANT TO RETURN WHAT WAS TAKEN FROM OUR FAMILY BEFORE I START MY OWN.
A GIRL.
I SEE A GIRL FOR YOU AND YOUR WIFE.
A GIRL?
SHE'S NEVER WRONG.
THANK YOU.

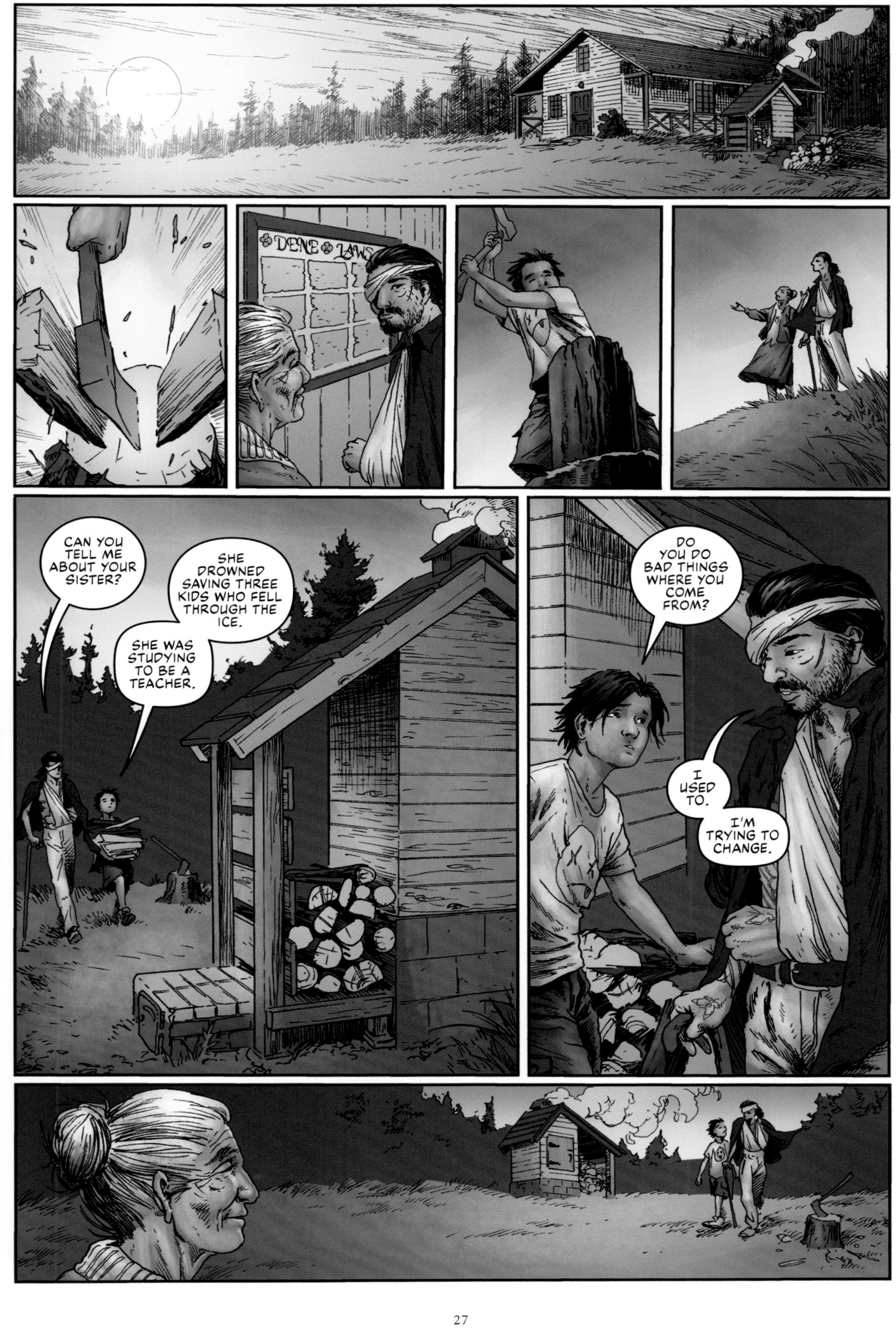
DENE LAWS
CAN YOU TELL ME ABOUT YOUR SISTER?
SHE DROWNED SAVING THREE KIDS WHO FELL THROUGH THE ICE.
SHE WAS STUDYING TO BE A TEACHER.
DO YOU DO BAD THINGS WHERE YOU COME FROM?
I USED TO.
I'M TRYING TO CHANGE.

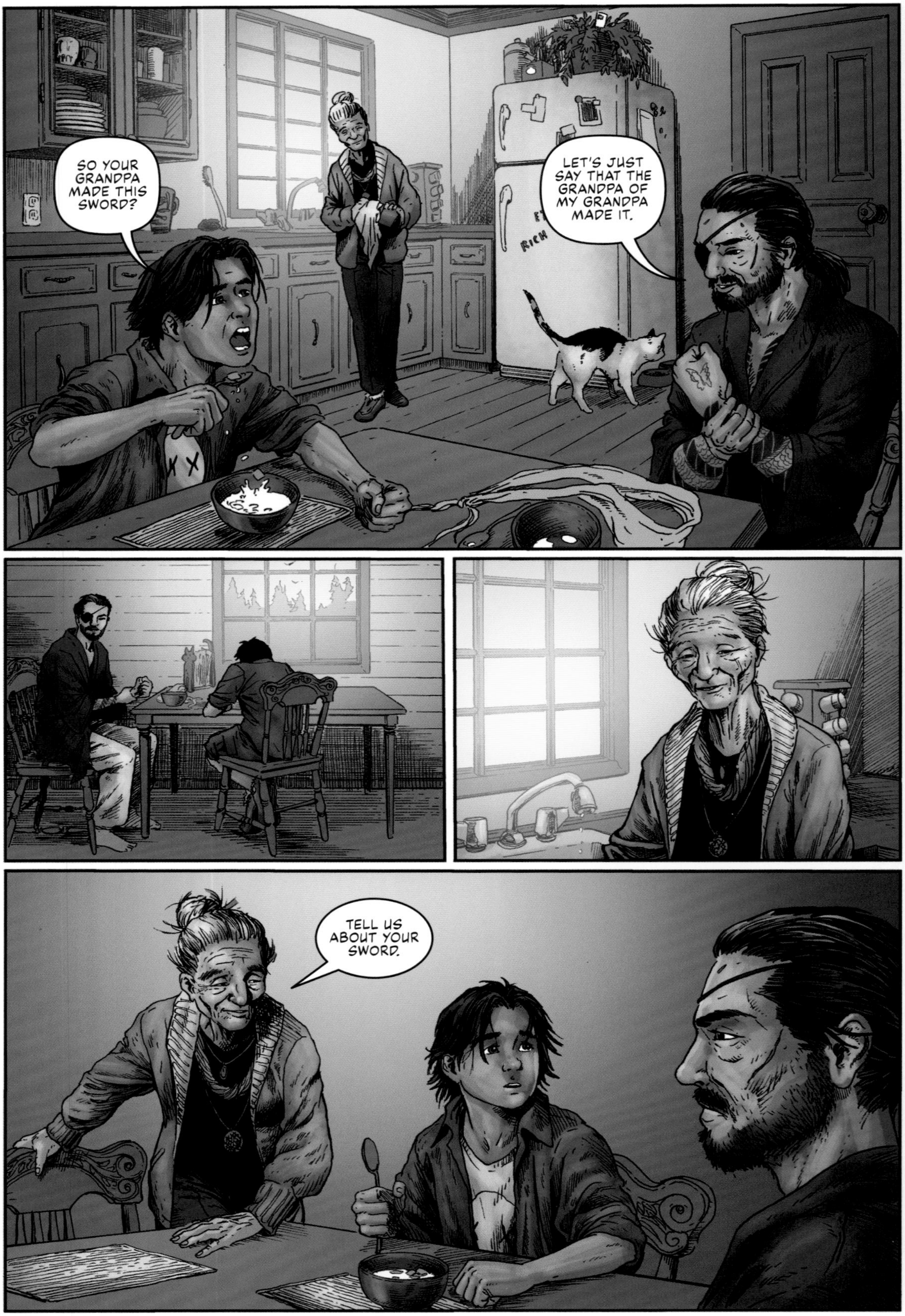
SO YOUR GRANDPA MADE THIS SWORD?
LET'S JUST SAY THAT THE GRANDPA OF MY GRANDPA MADE IT.
TELL US ABOUT YOUR SWORD.

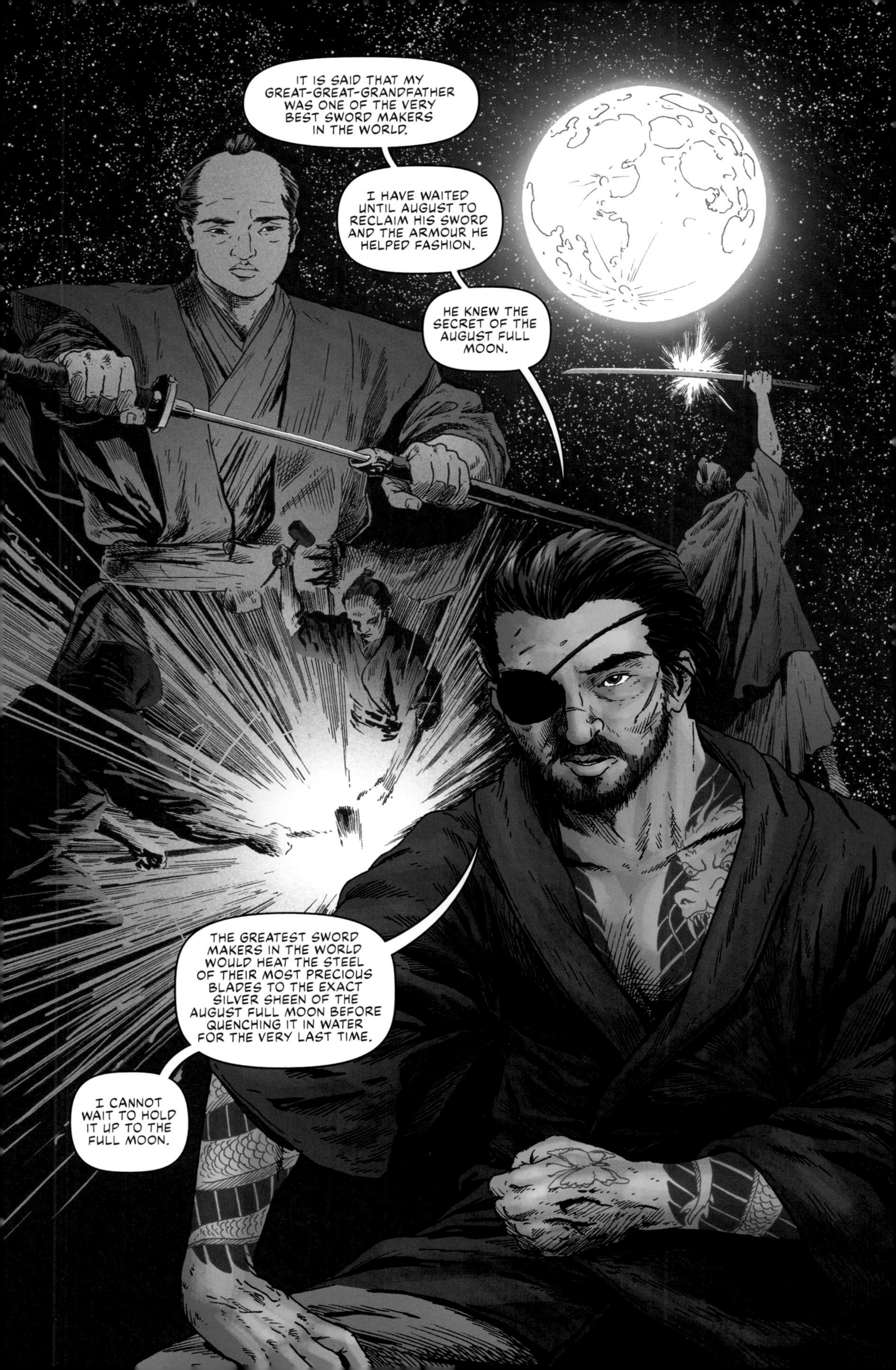
IT IS SAID THAT MY GREAT-GREAT-GRANDFATHER WAS ONE OF THE VERY BEST SWORD MAKERS IN THE WORLD.
I HAVE WAITED UNTIL AUGUST TO RECLAIM HIS SWORD AND THE ARMOUR HE HELPED FASHION.
HE KNEW THE SECRET OF THE AUGUST FULL MOON.
THE GREATEST SWORD MAKERS IN THE WORLD WOULD HEAT THE STEEL OF THEIR MOST PRECIOUS BLADES TO THE EXACT SILVER SHEEN OF THE AUGUST FULL MOON BEFORE QUENCHING IT IN WATER FOR THE VERY LAST TIME.
I CANNOT WAIT TO HOLD IT UP TO THE FULL MOON.

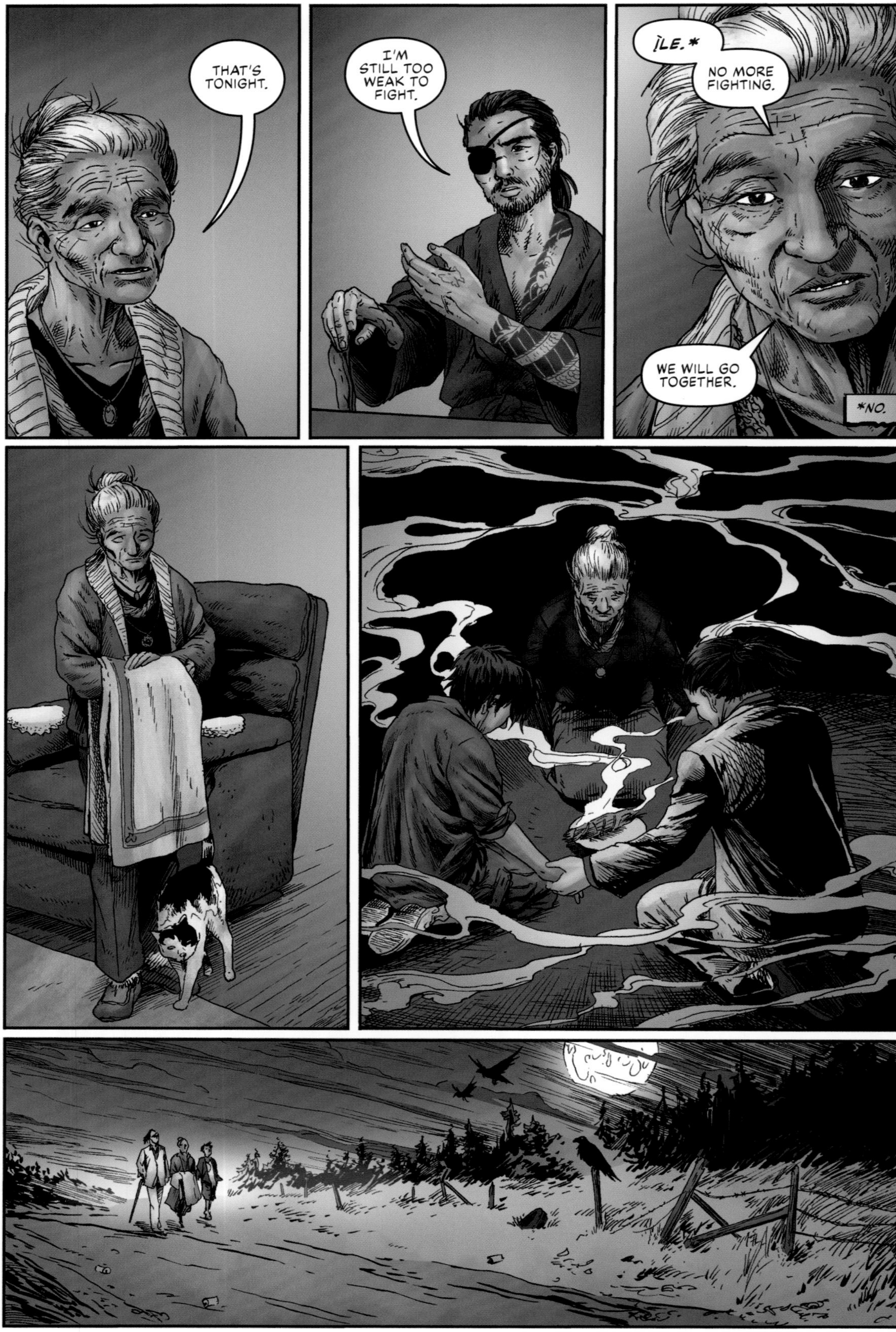
THAT'S TONIGHT.
I'M STILL TOO WEAK TO FIGHT.
ÌLE.*
NO MORE FIGHTING.
WE WILL GO TOGETHER.
*NO.

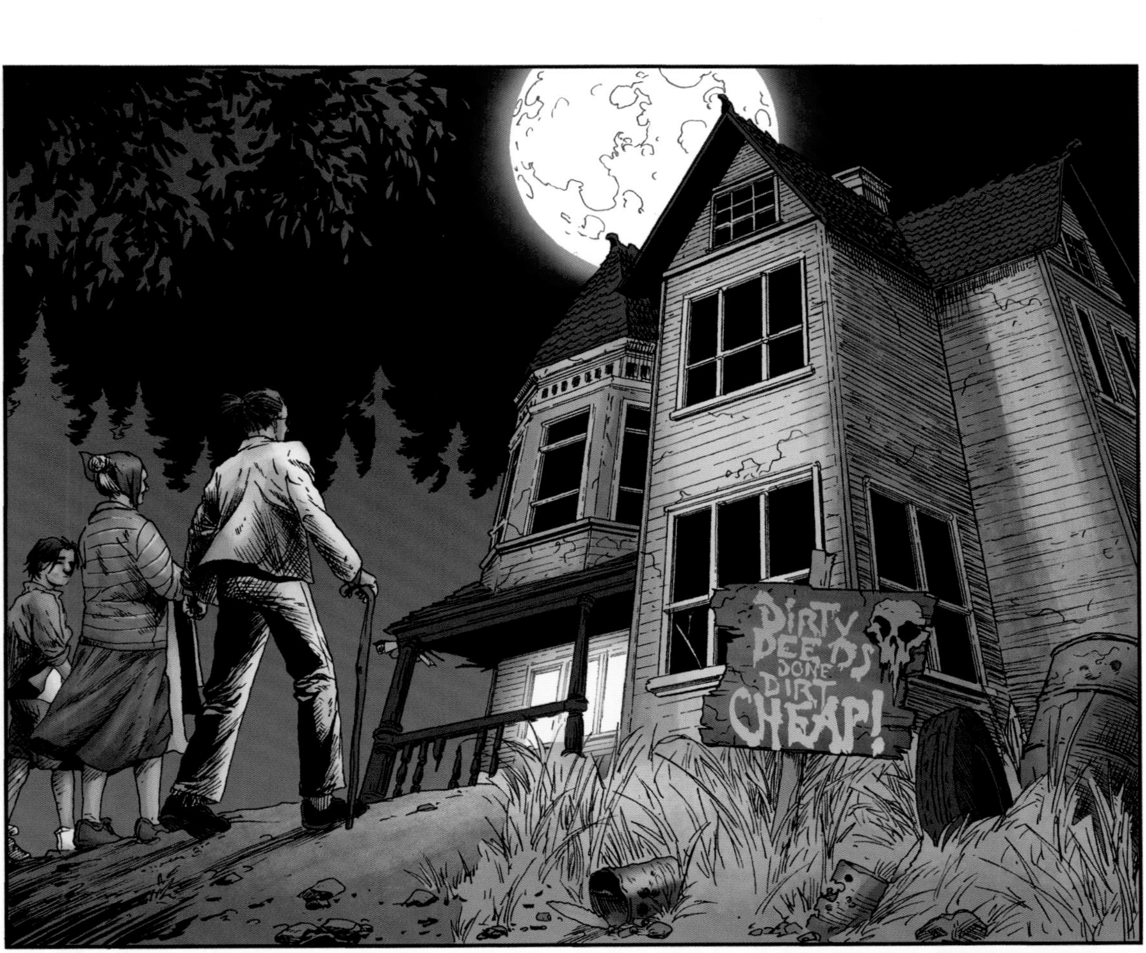
DIRTY DEEDS DONE DIRT CHEAP!
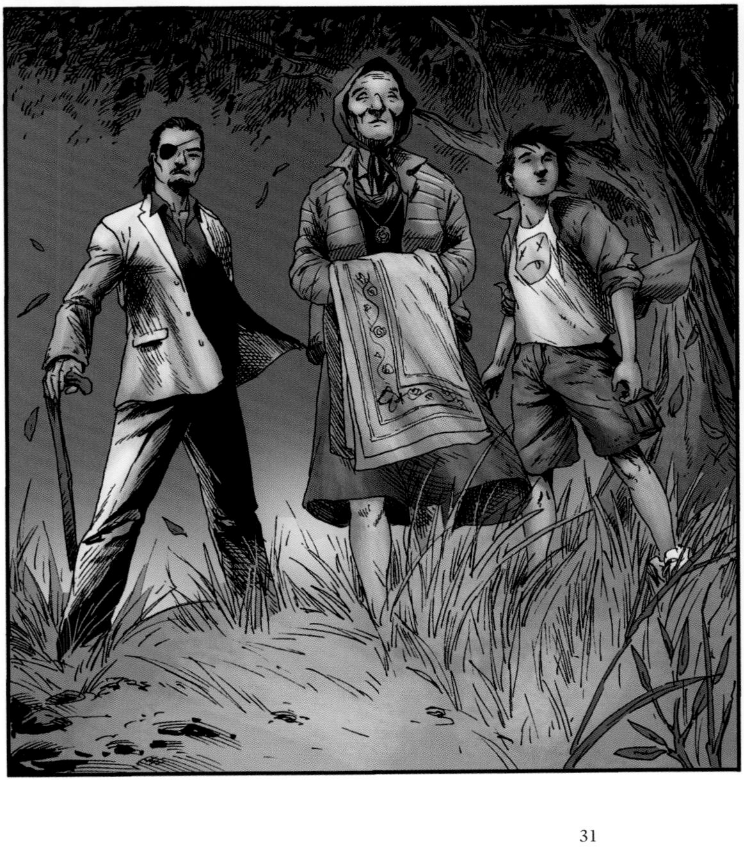
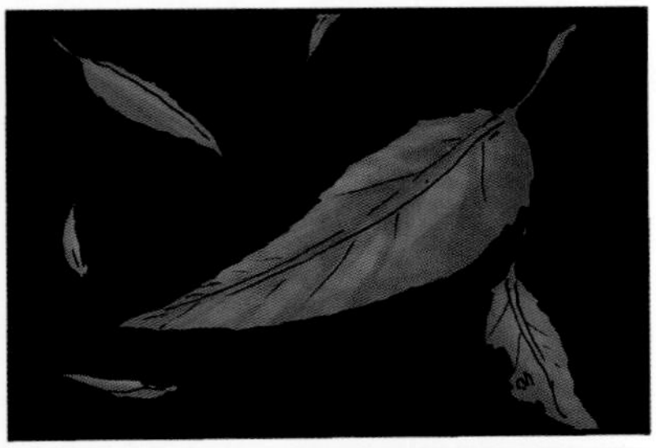
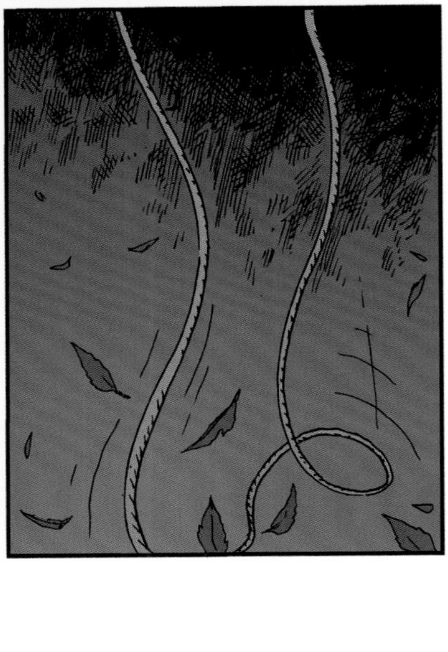

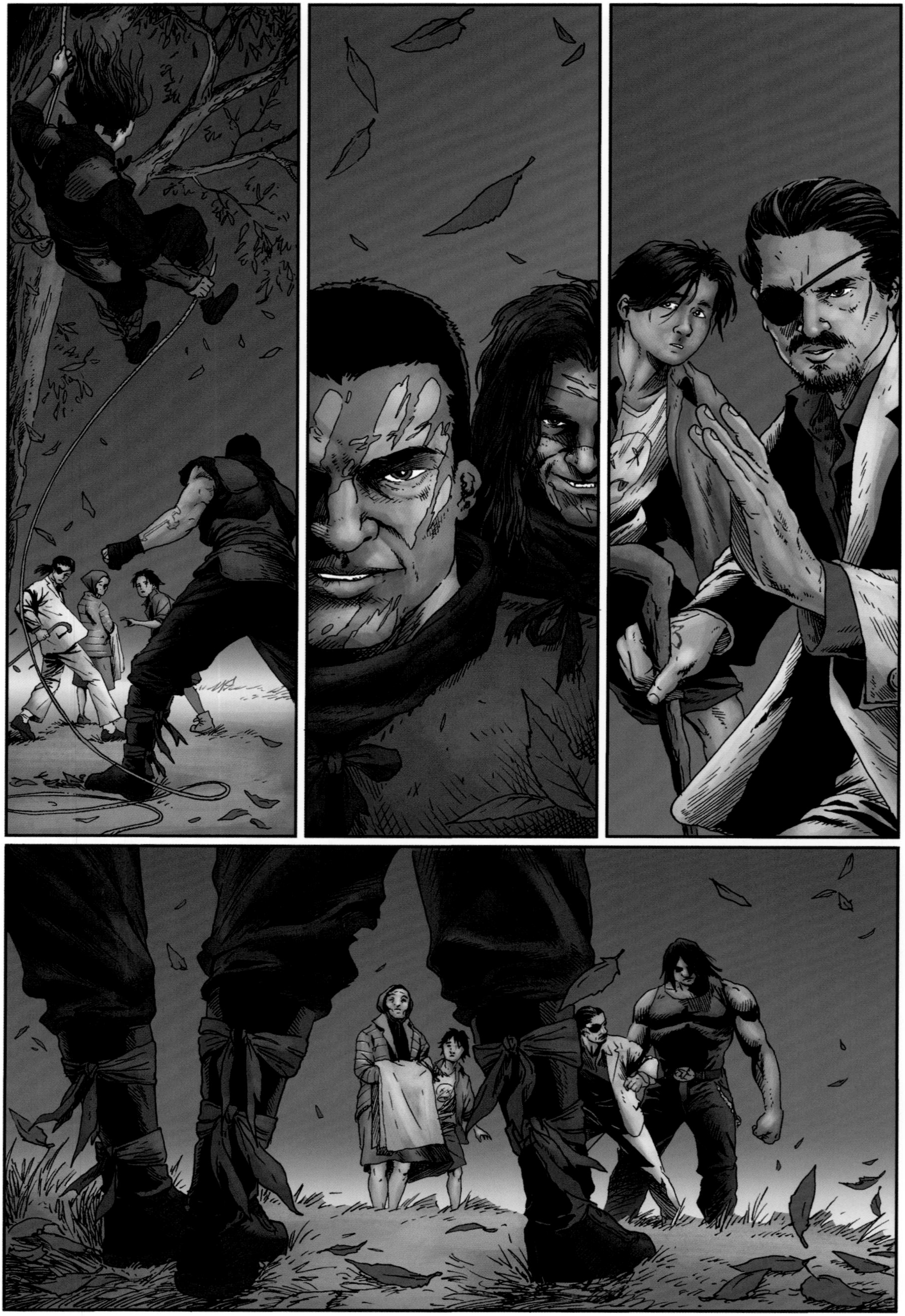

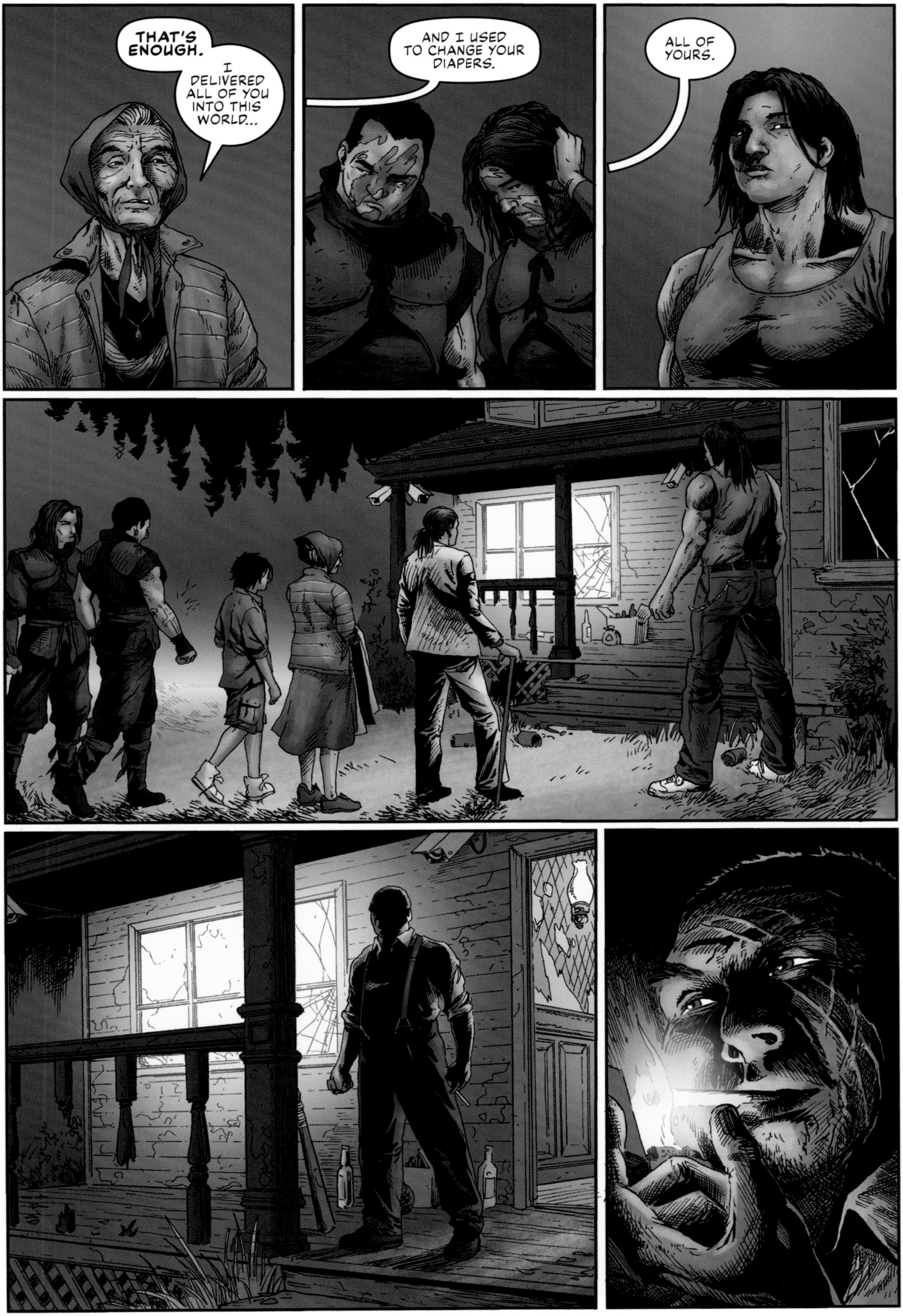
THAT'S ENOUGH.
I DELIVERED ALL OF YOU INTO THIS WORLD...
AND I USED TO CHANGE YOUR DIAPERS.
ALL OF YOURS.

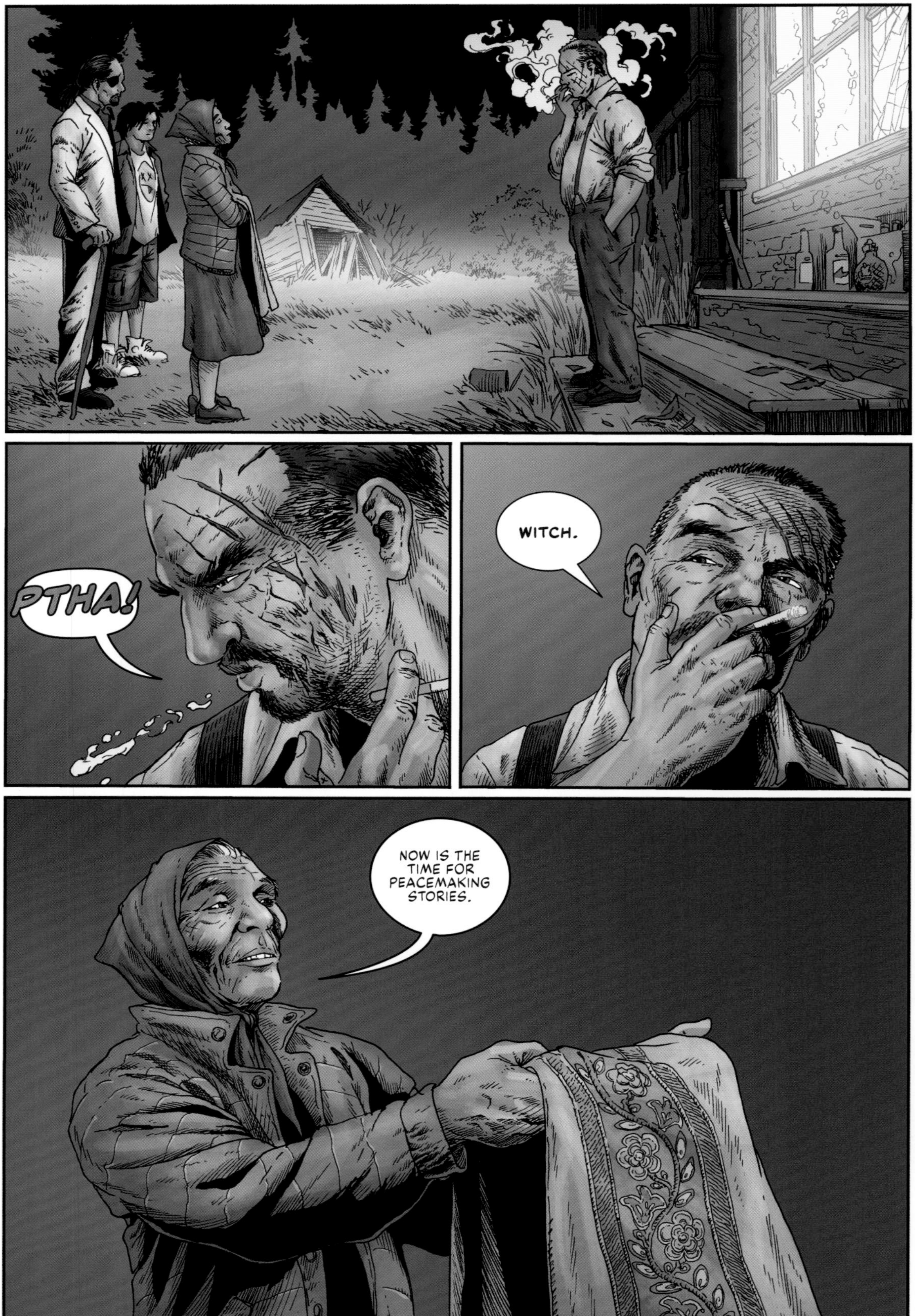
PTHA!
WITCH.
NOW IS THE TIME FOR PEACEMAKING STORIES.

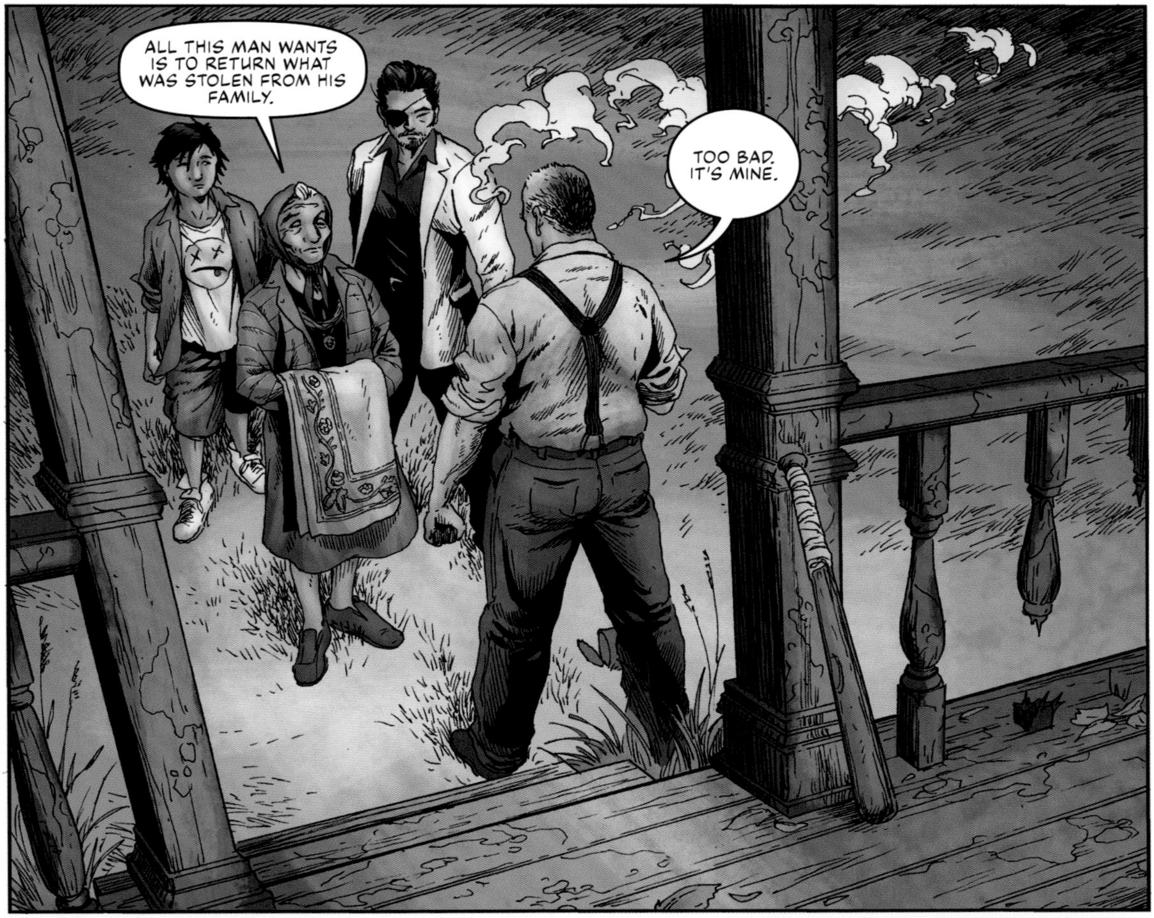
ALL THIS MAN WANTS IS TO RETURN WHAT WAS STOLEN FROM HIS FAMILY.
TOO BAD. IT'S MINE.

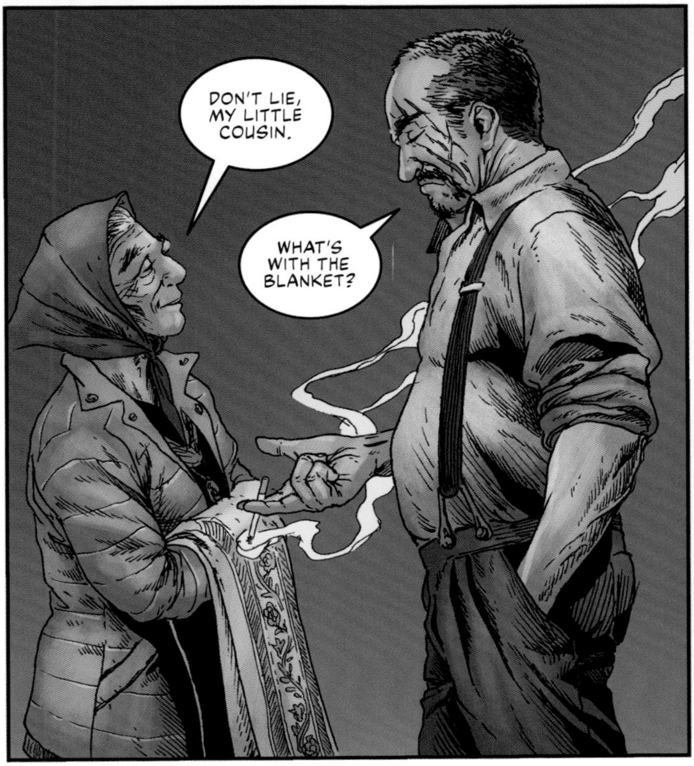
DON'T LIE, MY LITTLE COUSIN.
WHAT'S WITH THE BLANKET?

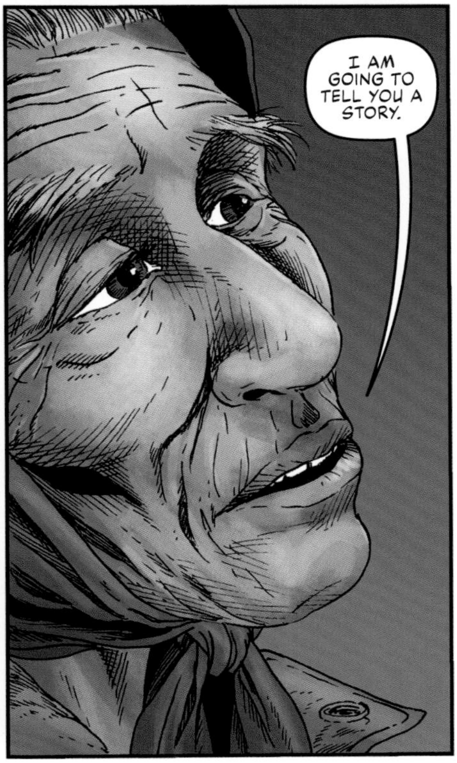
I AM GOING TO TELL YOU A STORY.

A LONG TIME AGO WHEN YOUR GRANDDAUGHTER WAS STRICKEN WITH CANCER, YOU ASKED ME TO HELP.

SOME PEOPLE CAN FIGHT WHAT SHE HAD. BUT SHE WAS TOO LITTLE.

SHE WAS ONLY SIX.

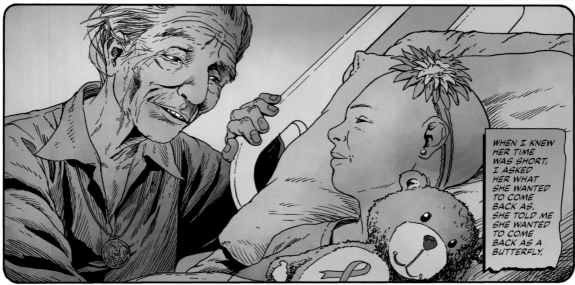

WHEN I KNEW HER TIME WAS SHORT, I ASKED HER WHAT SHE WANTED TO COME BACK AS. SHE TOLD ME SHE WANTED TO COME BACK AS A BUTTERFLY.

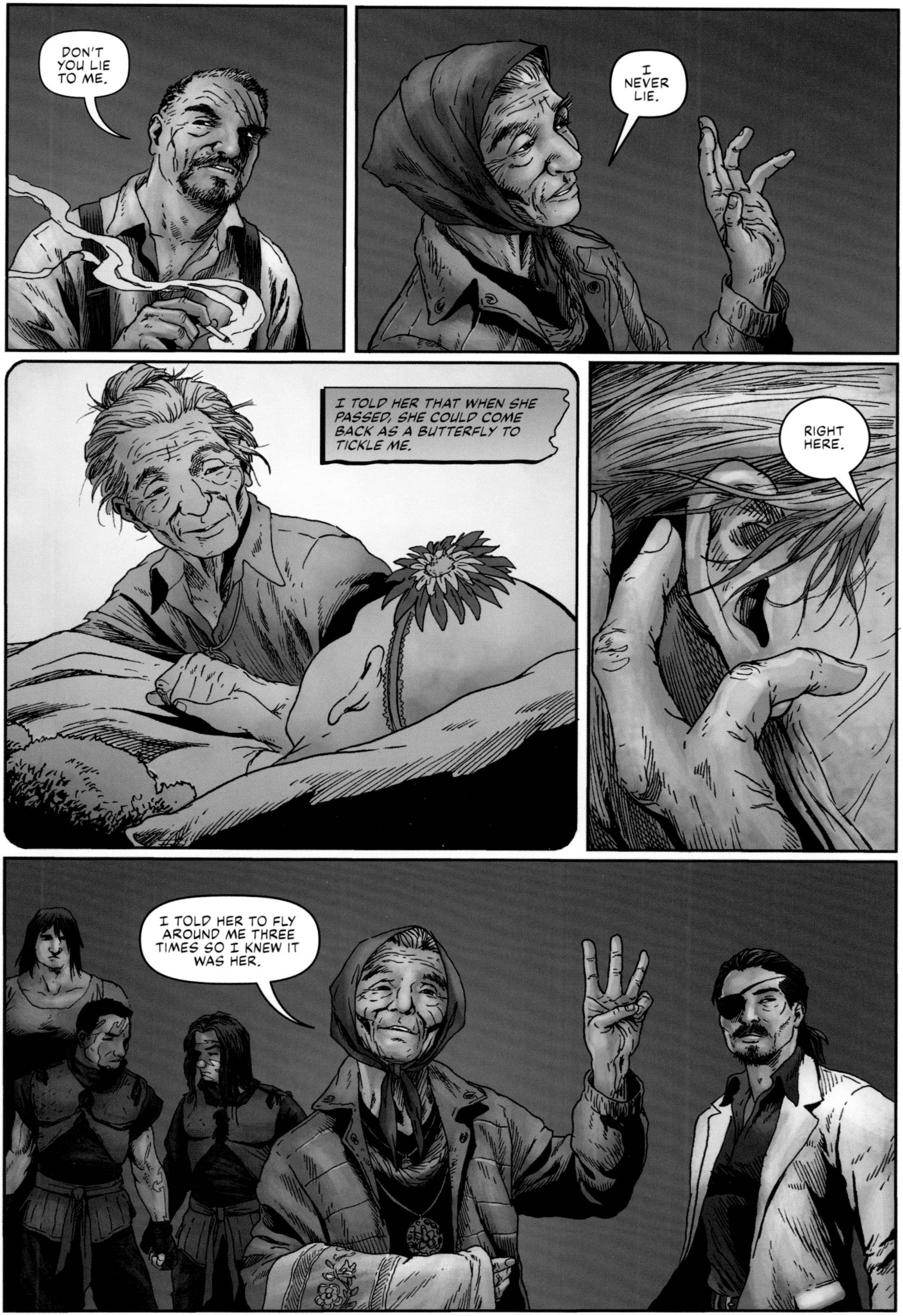
DON'T YOU LIE TO ME.
I NEVER LIE.
I TOLD HER THAT WHEN SHE PASSED, SHE COULD COME BACK AS A BUTTERFLY TO TICKLE ME.
RIGHT HERE.
I TOLD HER TO FLY AROUND ME THREE TIMES SO I KNEW IT WAS HER.

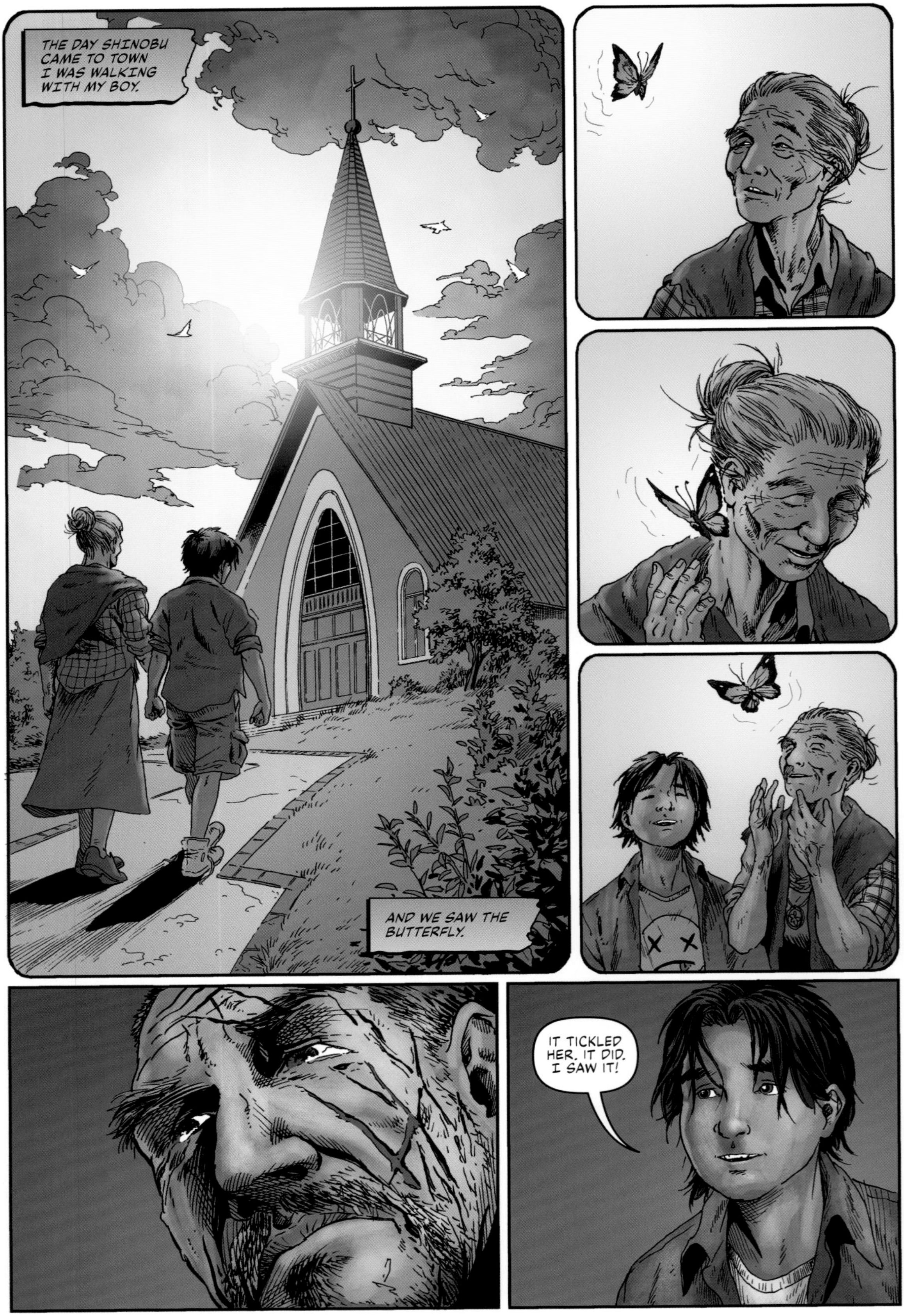
THE DAY SHINOBU CAME TO TOWN I WAS WALKING WITH MY BOY.
AND WE SAW THE BUTTERFLY.
IT TICKLED HER. IT DID. I SAW IT!

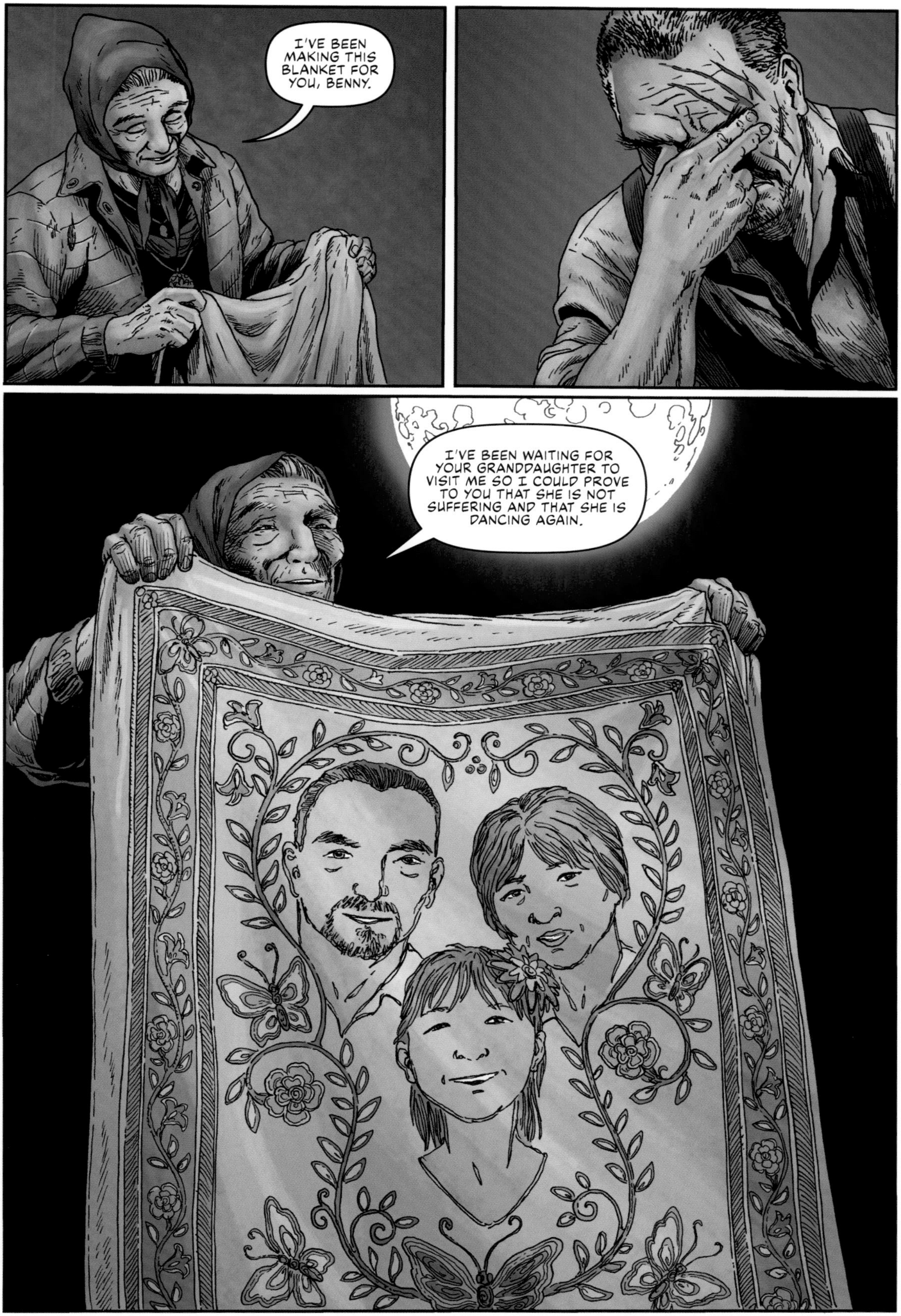
I'VE BEEN MAKING THIS BLANKET FOR YOU, BENNY.
I'VE BEEN WAITING FOR YOUR GRANDDAUGHTER TO VISIT ME SO I COULD PROVE TO YOU THAT SHE IS NOT SUFFERING AND THAT SHE IS DANCING AGAIN.

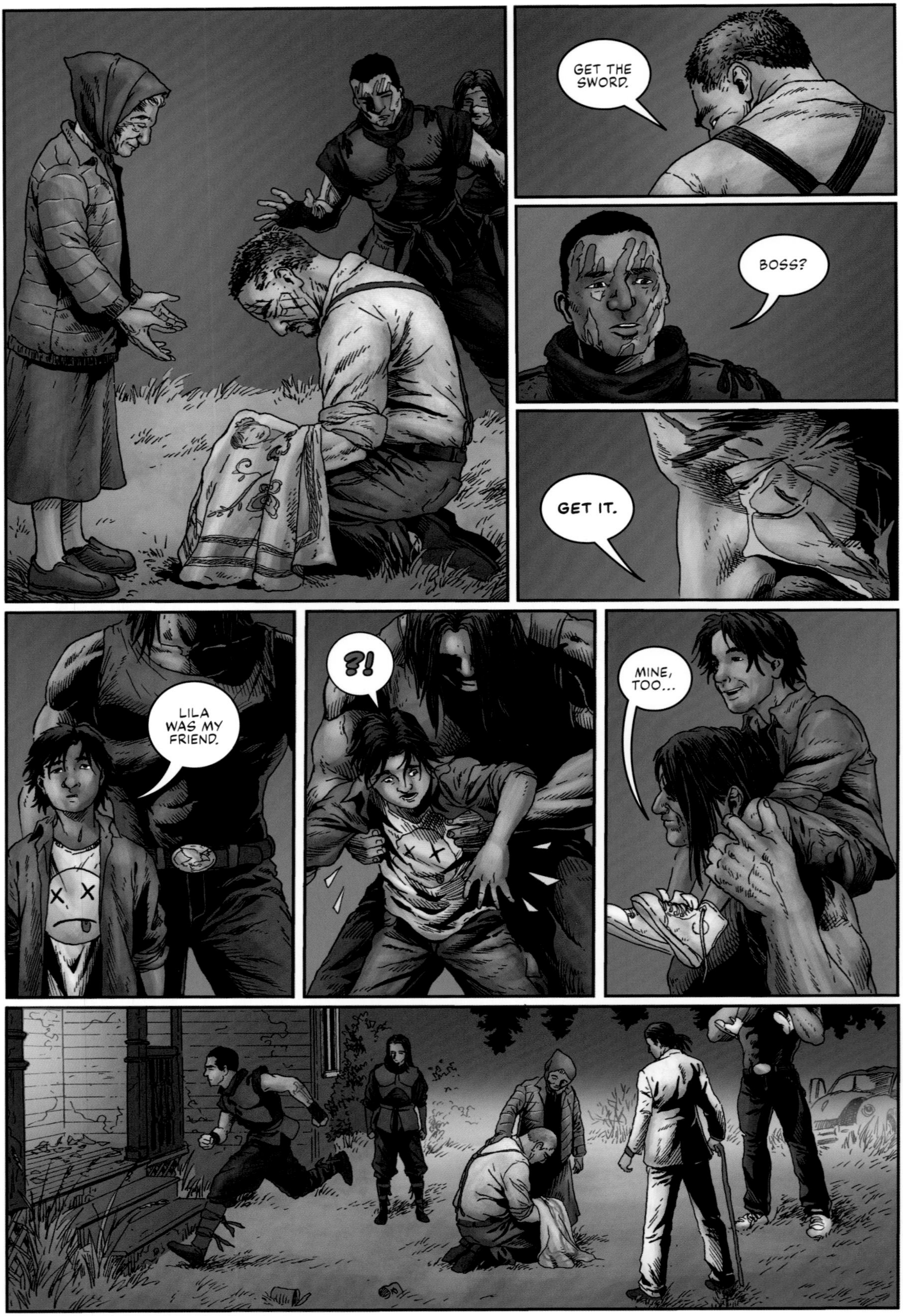
GET THE SWORD.
BOSS?
GET IT.
LILA WAS MY FRIEND.
?!
MINE, TOO...

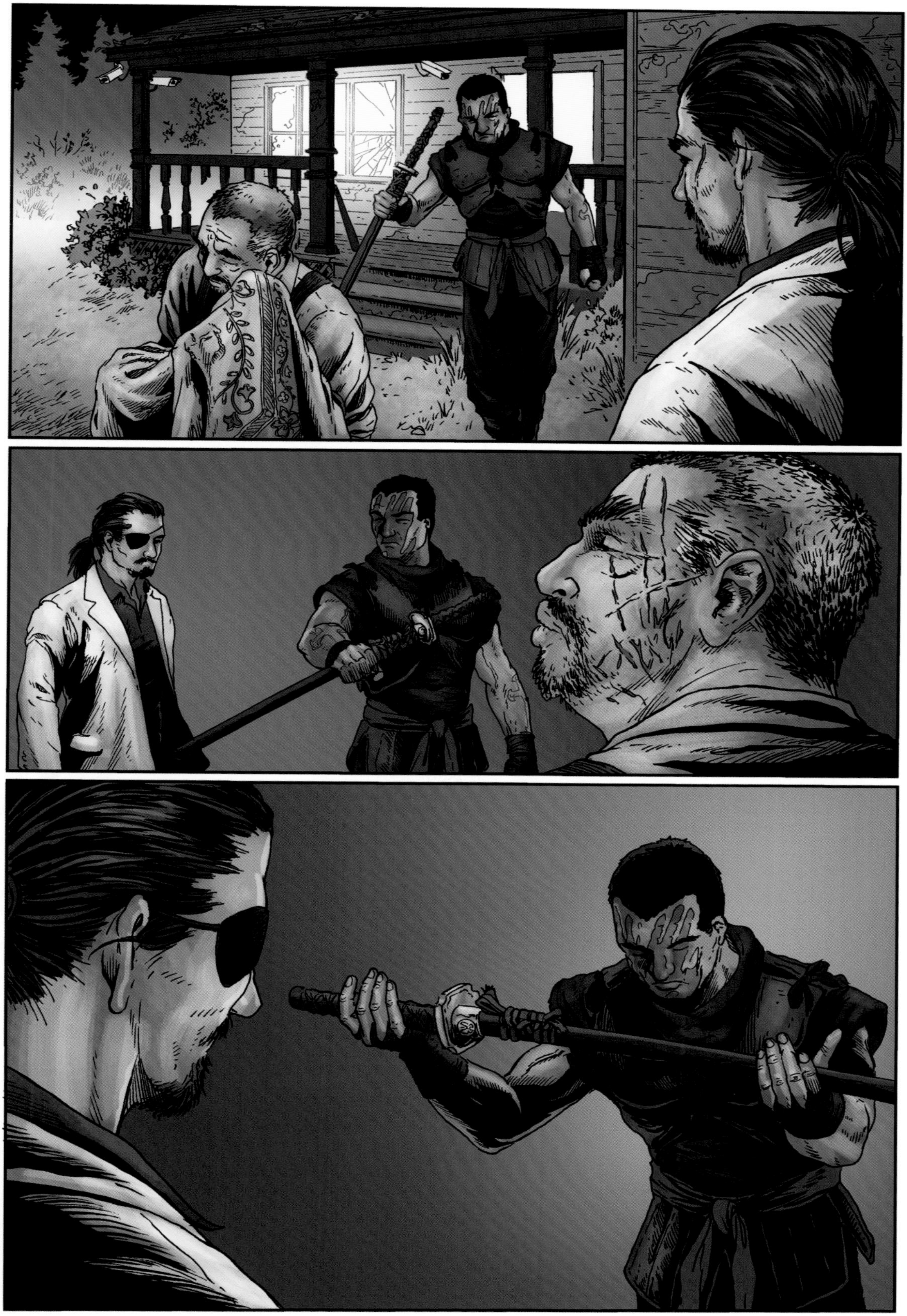

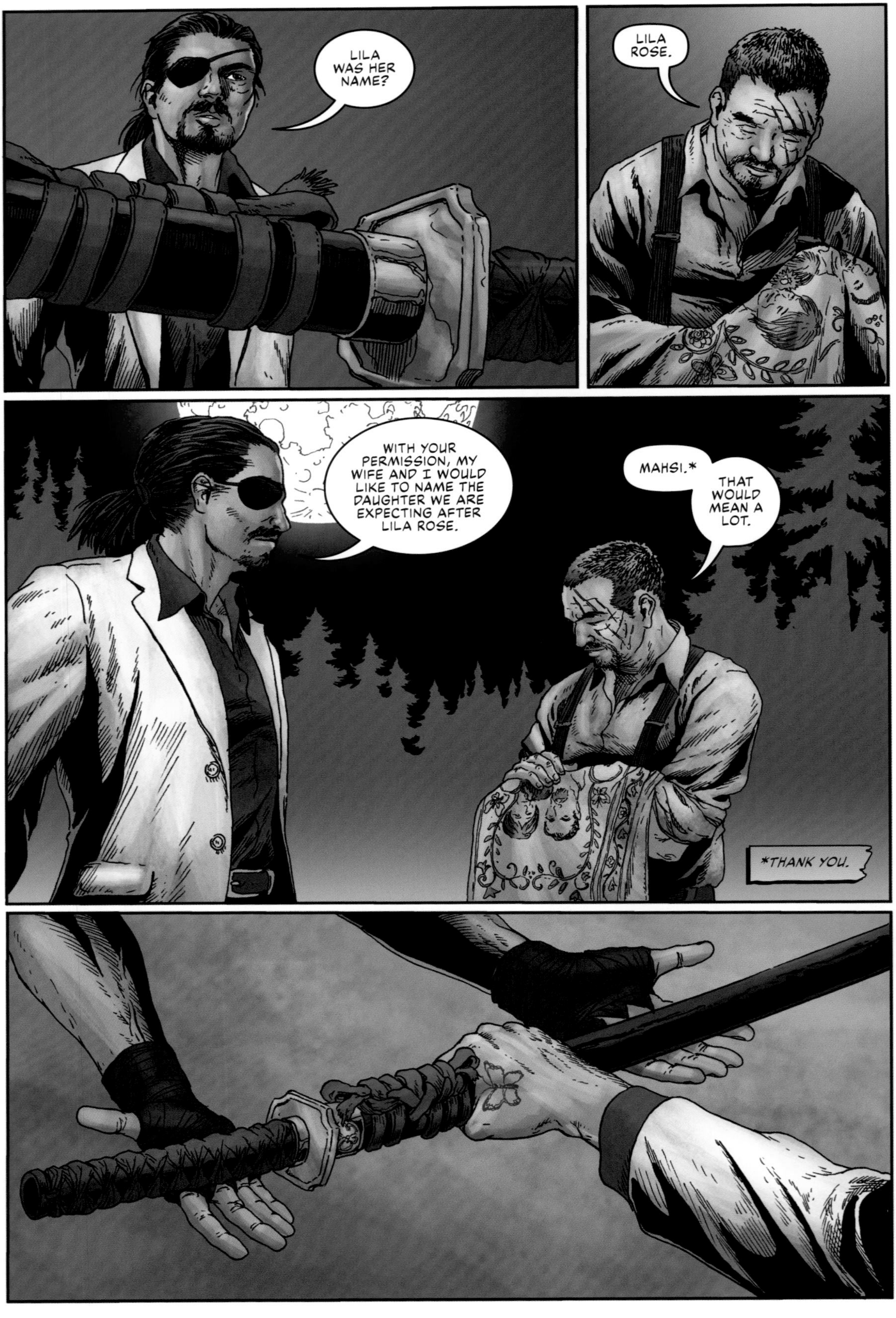
LILA WAS HER NAME?
LILA ROSE.
WITH YOUR PERMISSION, MY WIFE AND I WOULD LIKE TO NAME THE DAUGHTER WE ARE EXPECTING AFTER LILA ROSE.
MAHSI.*
THAT WOULD MEAN A LOT.
*THANK YOU.

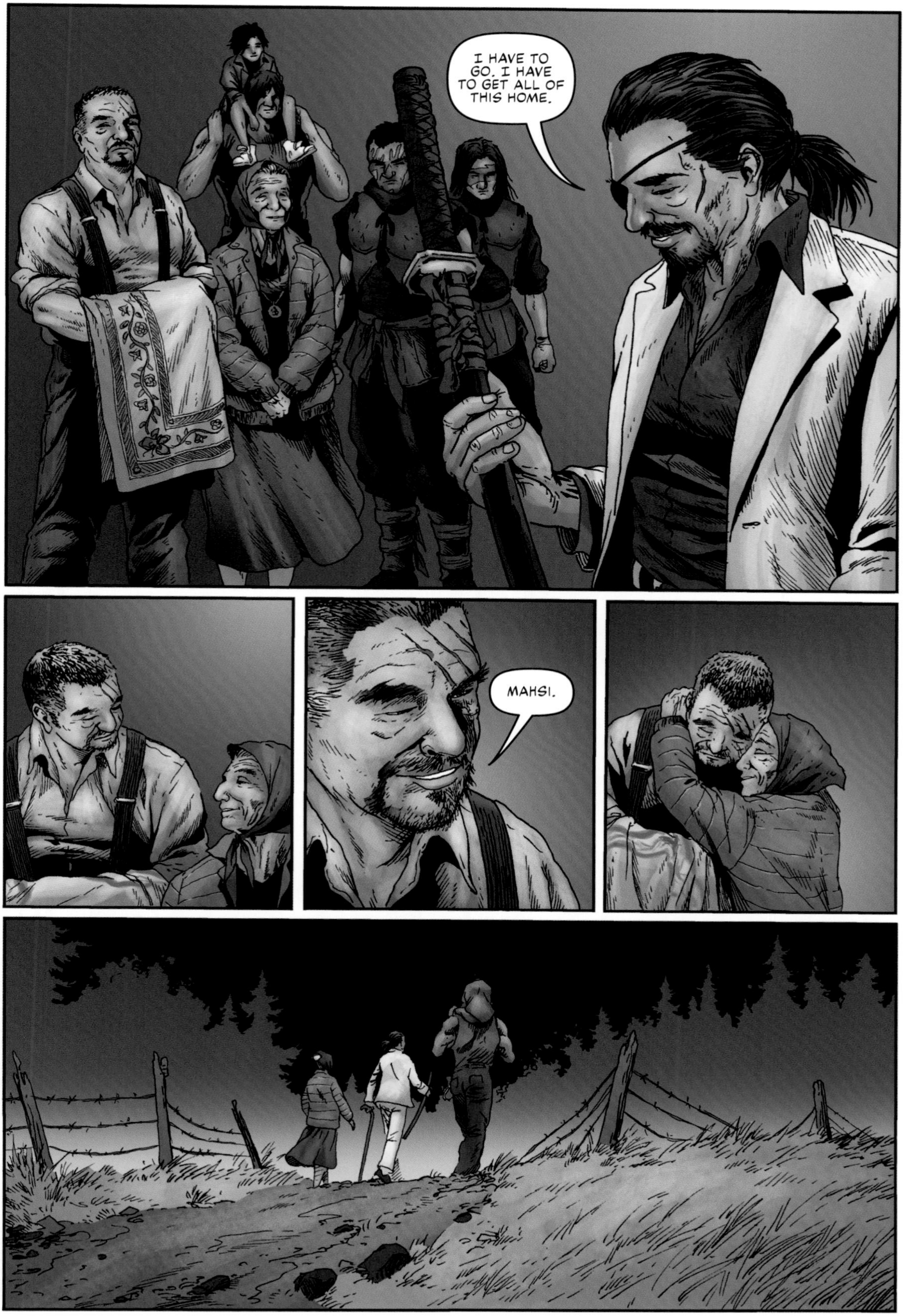
I HAVE TO GO. I HAVE TO GET ALL OF THIS HOME.
MAHSI.

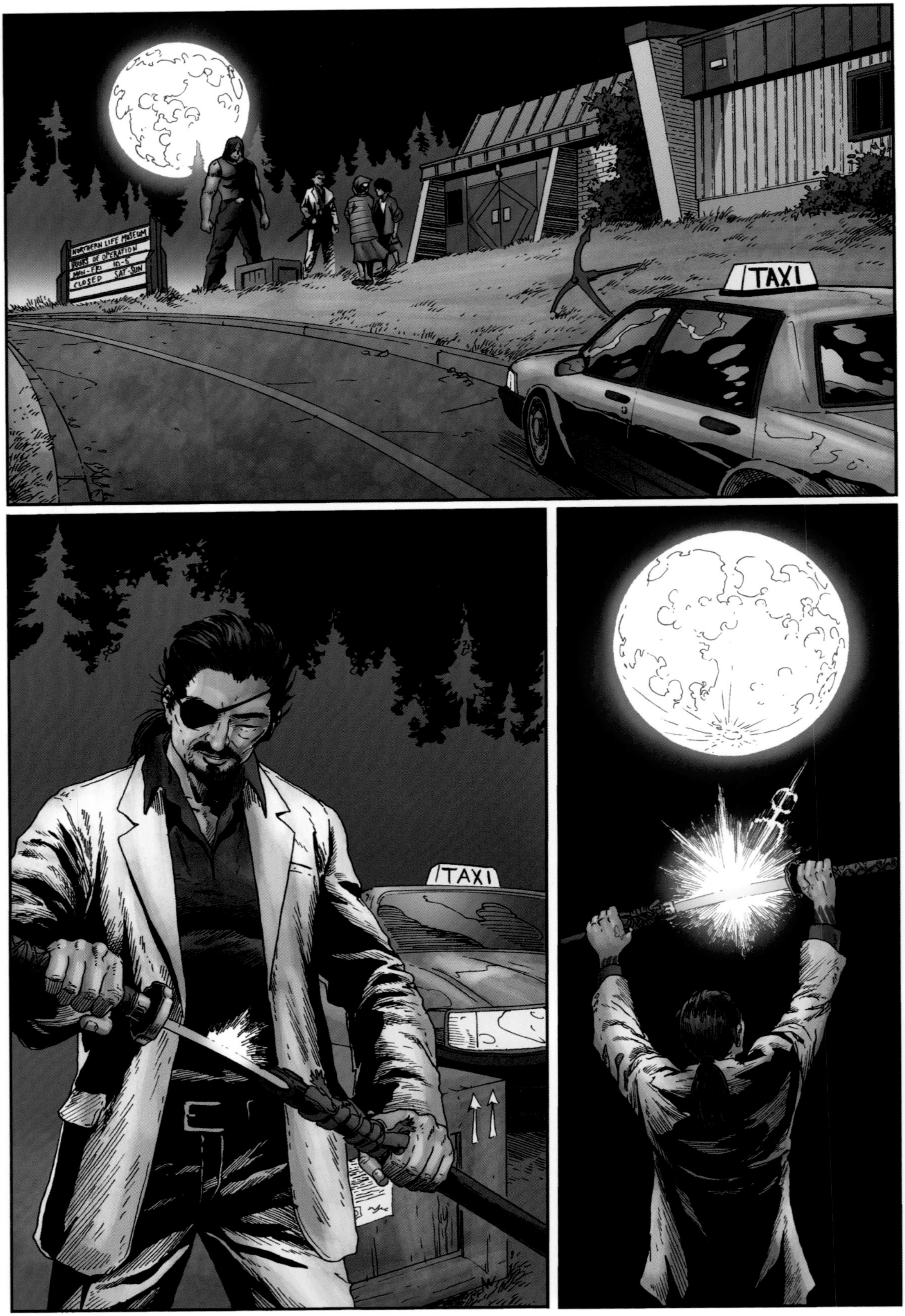
NORTHERN LIFE MUSEUM
HOURS OF OPERATION
MON-FRI 10-5
CLOSED SAT-SUN
TAXI
TAXI

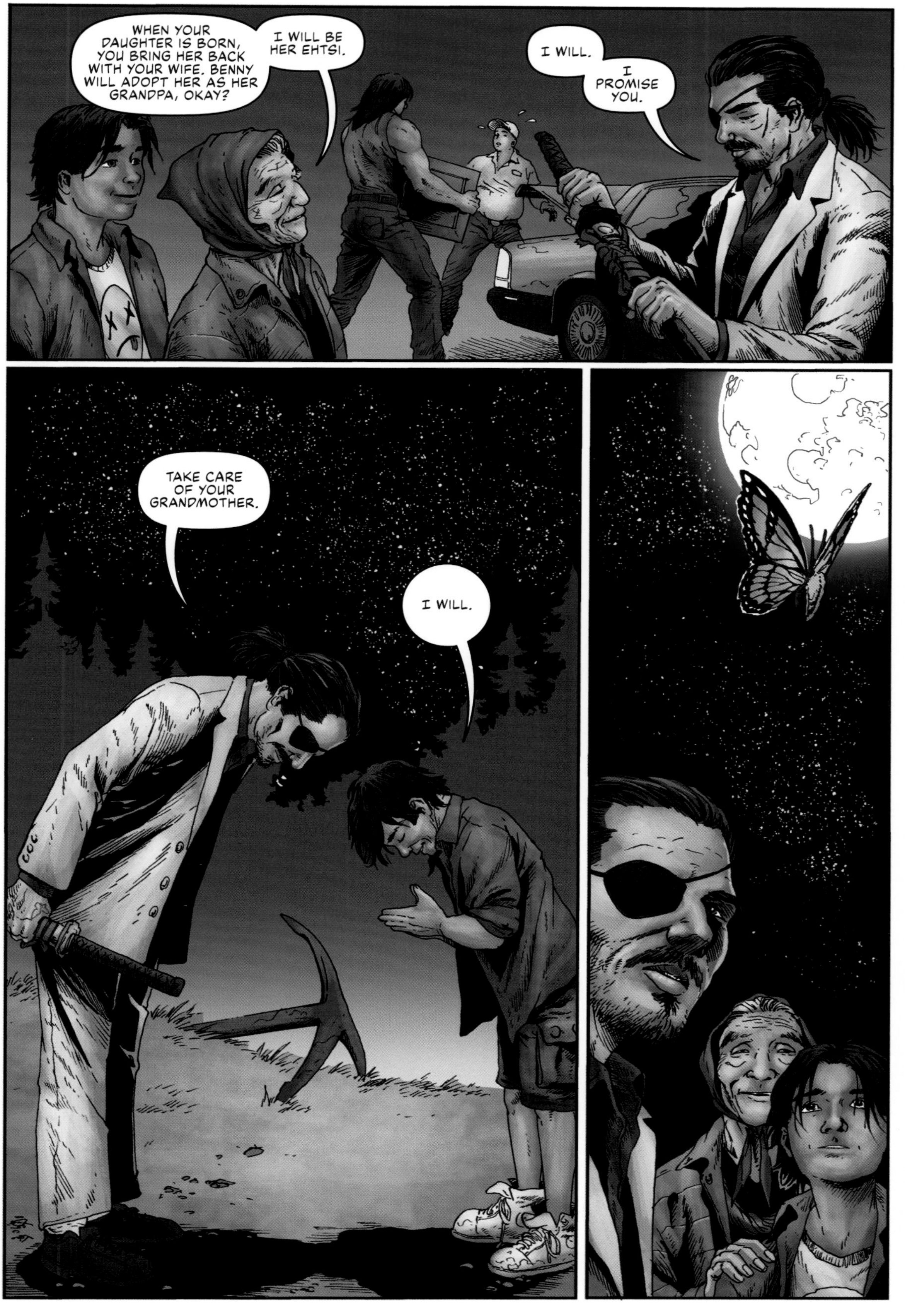
WHEN YOUR DAUGHTER IS BORN, YOU BRING HER BACK WITH YOUR WIFE. BENNY WILL ADOPT HER AS HER GRANDPA, OKAY?
I WILL BE HER EHTSI.
I WILL.
I PROMISE YOU.
TAKE CARE OF YOUR GRANDMOTHER.
I WILL.

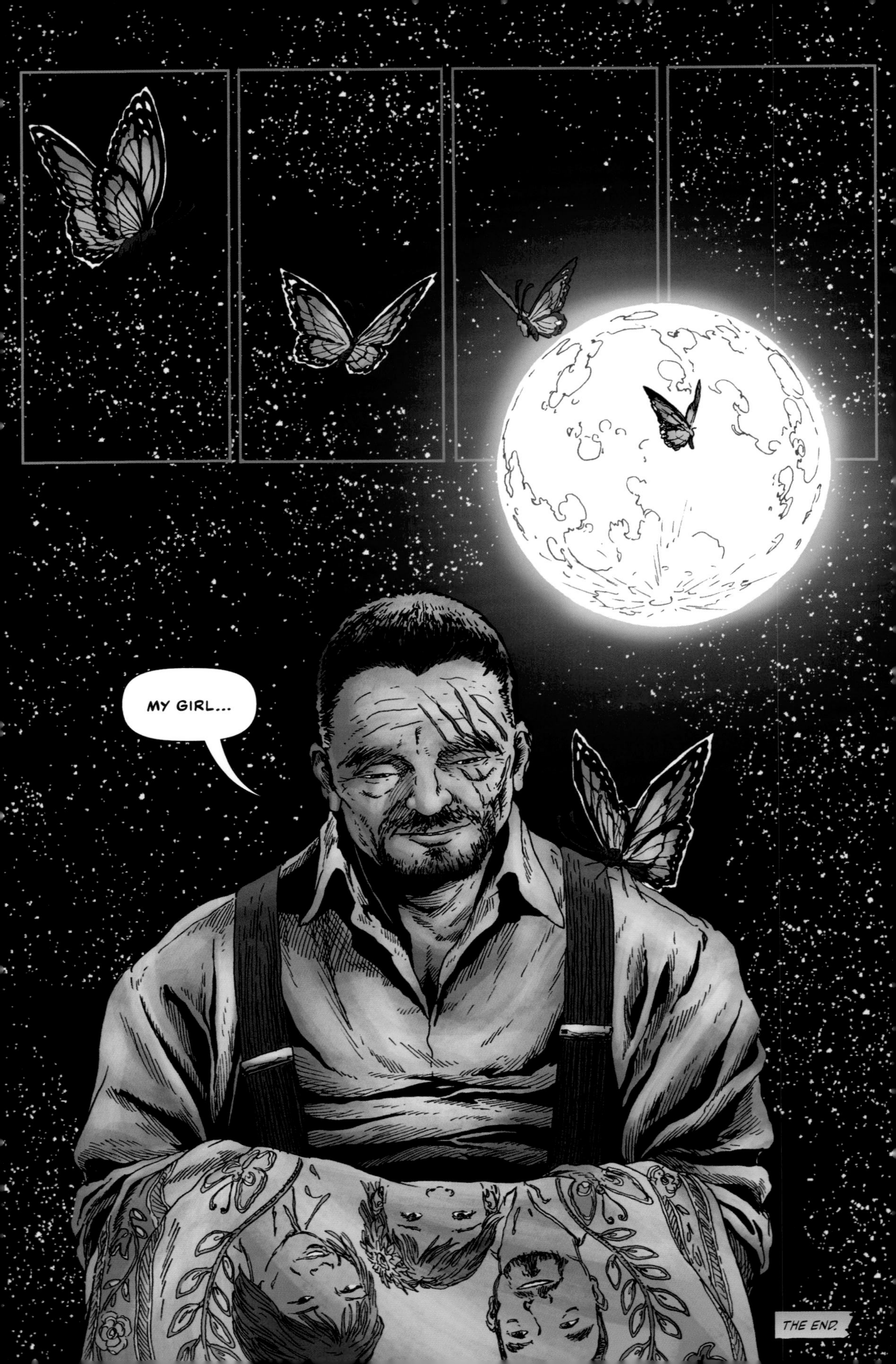
MY GIRL...
THE END.

The Second World War touched the lives of almost every person living in Canada, including many Indigenous peoples. Many thousands of Indigenous people volunteered for military service; others were conscripted, despite not having the right to vote. Relatively few Indigenous people from remote northern regions served in the military during the war. For the Dene in the Northwest Territories, the war was very far away and many felt it was not theirs to fight.

Nevertheless, that distant conflict came into their lands and lives in dramatic and damaging ways. Japan's strategic threat to Alaska and the North, as well as the need for natural resources like oil for the war effort, brought the government and the industrial world into remote northern regions that had previously been relatively isolated from southerners. Major defence projects such as the Alaska Highway and the Canol Pipeline, stretching from the oil fields in the Mackenzie Valley to Alaska, brought tens of thousands of American and Canadian military and civilian workers to the North. Even more workers were needed, however, and so Indigenous populations who already lived in these areas often found work guiding surveying crews or labouring on worksites.

The Manhattan Project was the code name for Allied governments' pursuit of atomic weapons. One fuel source for this weapons program was uranium, an uncommon radioactive element that the Allies could best access through deposits in the Great Bear Lake region of the Northwest Territories. A Crown corporation was established to mine the uranium and ship it south for processing. Wartime labour shortages in southern Canada forced mine operators to seek labour from local Dene communities to mine and haul the ore. At the time, there was a limited understanding of the dangers of handling radioactive substances and these workers had no protective clothing. As a result, the workers, and their families, were exposed to deadly levels of radiation and uranium toxicity. This led to high rates of cancer, kidney damage, impaired reproductive function, and chronic illness.

The damaging effects of these wartime activities continue to haunt many northern Indigenous communities to this day.

Dr. R. Scott Sheffield is the author of *The Red Man's on the Warpath: The Image of the "Indian" and the Second World War* and *Indigenous Peoples and the Second World War: The Politics, Experiences and Legacies of the War in the US, Canada, Australia and New Zealand* (with Noah Riseman).

The armour of Shinobu's forebears resembles one in our collection at the Nikkei National Museum. Our mission is to honour, preserve, and share the history and heritage of Japanese Canadians and Japanese culture in Canada. Although we believe the armour to be from the Hikone samurai clan in Japan, we do not know how it came to Canada, or any more information about the family for whom it must have been a precious heirloom. We do know that a Vancouver artist, Robert Samuel Alexander, bought it in a thrift shop sometime before 1951. We believe that it was taken from a Japanese Canadian family who was forced to leave the West Coast in 1942.

1942 was the year the Canadian government ordered all "persons of Japanese racial origin"[1] to leave their homes in a so-called evacuation. The Canadian government implied a security threat from Canada's war with Japan as the reason.[2] However, experts in the RCMP and the Canadian military had already told the government that this uprooting was not necessary. Japanese Canadians were no security threat.

But Japanese Canadians had to follow the orders to leave the coast. There were strict limits on the baggage they were allowed to carry. The government also promised to hold any property left behind in trust until they were able to return.[3] With this assurance, and without other choices, many families left behind priceless heirlooms in their homes. After they left, many Japanese Canadians' homes were looted. Beginning in 1943, the Canadian government sold all remaining Japanese Canadian property that it had been holding in trust at auction.

In *A Blanket of Butterflies*, Shinobu travels from Japan to reclaim his family's armour and sword. Perhaps they too were Canadian thrift store finds. They could have been taken from one of the thousands of Japanese Canadians whom the Canadian government exiled to Japan in 1946. Shinobu may have had a Canadian-born parent or grandparent who taught him English, or perhaps this is his family's first journey to North America.

In the fallout from the Second World War, many Japanese descendants of samurai were prisoners of war or even defendants in trials for war crimes. Members of the Allied forces overseeing these trials sometimes had access to prisoners' confiscated items, such as swords and perhaps armour. This is another historical possibility for how the armour and sword in *A Blanket of Butterflies* ended up in Canada, en route to Arkansas.

Shinobu's tattooed body hints that his reclaiming of the armour and sword is also a story of personal redemption. In Japan, tattoos are considered the domain of yakuza members (Japanese gangsters). They are taboo to the point of being forbidden in public hot springs and baths.

Shinobu's quest to recover his family's material history from far-flung places is one that a great many Japanese Canadians, and I imagine at least as many Indigenous people, can relate to. It is no surprise to me that the Dene community in this story made no attempt to redirect these heirlooms to their intended destination, but instead persistently sought out their rightful cultural owners.

Carolyn Nakagawa
Education Program Developer
Nikkei National Museum & Cultural Centre

1 Order-in-Council P.C. 1486—February 24, 1942
2 Order-in-Council P.C. 1486—February 24, 1942
3 Order-in-Council P.C. 1665—March 4, 1942